UNHONORED

UNHONORED

BOOK TWO *of* THE NIGHTBIRDS

Tracy Hickman &
Laura Hickman

A TOM DOHERTY ASSOCIATES BOOK
NEW YORK

UNHONORED

Copyright © 2016 by Tracy Hickman and Laura Hickman

A Tor Book
Published by Tom Doherty Associates
175 Fifth Avenue
New York, NY 10010

www.tor-forge.com

Tor® is a registered trademark of Macmillan Publishing Group, LLC.

The Library of Congress Cataloging-in-Publication Data
is available upon request.

ISBN 978-0-7653-3204-2 (hardcover)
ISBN 978-1-4299-5333-7 (e-book)

Our books may be purchased in bulk for promotional, educational, or business use. Please contact your local bookseller or the Macmillan Corporate and Premium Sales Department at 1-800-221-7945, extension 5442, or by e-mail at MacmillanSpecialMarkets@macmillan.com.

First Edition: October 2016

Printed in the United States of America

0 9 8 7 6 5 4 3 2 1

CONTENTS

The opposite of love is not hate,
it's indifference.
The opposite of art is not ugliness,
it's indifference.
The opposite of faith is not heresy,
it's indifference.
And the opposite of life is not death,
it's indifference.

—Elie Wiesel

UNHONORED

1

HOUSE OF DREAMS

Margaret Emma Kendrick stood shaking in the endless, dark space.

She sensed there was floor beneath her boot-shod feet and felt the rough cloth of the dress draped over her. There was nothing else that existed and while she dreaded the suffocating nature of the experience, she had also come to expect the same. It served her best, she knew, to hold perfectly still, to try not to move and to wait for the new world to appear.

She perceived more than saw the mirror gathering itself together before her and shuddered.

She did not want to look at the demon in the glass, another self on the far side of the reflection. She imagined it to be a terrible thing, a monstrous version of herself that was biding its time, waiting, somehow, to reach through the glass and tear her life from her throat. Worse still, she was unsure which of them was the real Margaret and which of them was merely the reflection.

This was the part that she hated the most: the dreaded aspect of coming into being. She wondered vaguely if this was what birth was like: emerging in horror from the darkness into a new existence. She had no experience to answer such a question, she mused, for she had never been born.

Yet she had done this before. She had been banished to the Umbra more times than she could count and returned to play again when a new Day was decreed. Each time, emerging from the nothingness into a parody of living had unsettled her. She enjoyed playing at life but she hated starting to live. She dreaded being recalled from the sim-plicity of nothingness. Coming into being terrified her every time.

Her eyes perceived shadows emerging from the noth-ing around her, giving shape to the oval mirror before her. An outline of a figure stared back at her from the glass. It was a vague and faceless outline. Margaret filled in its features with her imagination and still could not stop herself from shaking.

The woman staring back at her, quivering in the near darkness, was plain-faced and careworn. Her red hair was pulled back from her square face and braided at the back in what Margaret considered a careless manner. Her green eyes bulged slightly and seemed to stare back at her as though daring her to wish she were different from who she had become. At least she had kept her red hair. She found it difficult to look at her reflection as she trembled in the flickering light of a lantern that was becoming more real as it brightened next to her.

The drab dress. The effort to carry her shoulders back and her carriage erect against the weight of her station. She had hoped to be more this time—so much more—but the Book decreed the parts that each of them must play. Her position and false memories came to her then, rising up from somewhere beyond conscious thought and helping her know who she was to be in this life, this new Day.

She knew her part. She was a servant. A lady's maid and that was not the worst of it.

She was a lady's maid to *her*.

Margaret clenched her teeth at the thought. *Her* of all people.

"Margaret Emma Kendrick," she murmured to her image reflected in the mirror. "It's going to be a hard Day."

Margaret reached down and picked up the lamp. As she held it higher, the extent of the room around her became evident. She did not know nor particularly care whether the walls had been there all along or whether they came into being when she looked for them. Such considerations, she grimly thought, were above her station. It was her servants' quarters, barely more than a closet in many ways with just enough room for the mirror, her narrow bed and a chest of drawers. There was even a window, although the panes of glass were so black with darkness that they looked as though they had been painted with it.

She wondered, quite rightly, if there was anything beyond the glass as yet.

Margaret turned toward the door that had appeared opposite where the bed lay and, impulsively, reached for the handle. Suddenly she hesitated, her fingers poised to grasp the tarnished brass knob but stopping short of closing around it. *Is there the house beyond?* she thought in a sudden panic. *Has it returned as it was before she left us or is there nothing but a void across this threshold?*

She glanced downward toward the floor and the gap beneath the door. A dim, warm light was brightening there.

Margaret drew in a deep breath, held it, and then opened the door.

There was a poorly lit hallway beyond, undecorated and lined with plain doors on either side. The hall was lit with feeble gas jets flickering at intervals from where they hung in fixtures from the ceiling. At the near end of the corridor, Margaret could make out a tight staircase leading down into the house. As she turned to look down the hallway in the other direction, she could see that the light from the gas jets ended just twenty feet from where she stood with her own lamp still in her hand. Beyond there the walls became vague and shadowed, falling away into impenetrable nothingness. As she watched, the gas jet in the next fixture sprang to life with a soft chuffing sound, pushing back the darkness and revealing more of the corridor. Moment by deliberate moment, the ceiling fixtures puffed into life and with each increased illumination brought more of the corridor into existence.

"Echo House," Margaret muttered to herself. "A new name for so old a place. So you are awakening at last. How long have you slept in our memory?"

Margaret turned back toward the stairs and peered down over the railing. The staircase ran downward and then ended in a solid wall with an ornate pane of Tiffany glass. It was completely without reason for the downward staircase to end in a wall yet, Margaret reflected, that was the nature of the house.

This place was familiar to her. She had been here before. She had played a different part then and far more suited to her liking but the house . . . Oh, yes, the house she knew all too well.

Margaret sighed. She was not yet used to the way she looked or the new role that she had to play. She was happy, if such a term could be used about her, to have any part at all in this new life. Merrick had been very clear to her about that. This was her part in the Day and she would accept her position or have no life at all.

She closed her eyes. She had been a princess once, the focus of suitors' and courtiers' attentions and by her command those who had offended her had been banished. She had been a lady-in-waiting of a great empire, too, and at her word gladiators had received their final blow. When the harbor town had become the Game, she had clawed her way up the society of Gamin and had often been a serious contender to beat them all, take control of the Day, and make her own Book.

But she had always been a princess, never been the queen; a lady-in-waiting but never empress. She had always stood in the shadow of someone else, never to glory in the light of the Day.

That was always that *other* woman's role.

Now a new Day had dawned. Merrick had decreed it and she and the others had been pulled from the blissful nothingness into another Game, another pretense.

For Margaret, another chance.

She heard a growing sound roiling up from the far end of the hall. The echo of laughter, the thudding tread of feet and the muffled sound of indistinct words. Margaret held her lamp high as she moved down the hall. She passed the closed doors on either side—most likely more servants' quarters although, she mused, Merrick had never been particularly careful about the sensibility of his own architecture. The gas jets flared to life before her, revealing, or creating, more hallway in front of her as she walked. Still, she clung to the lamp for she knew that every door before her could still open onto darkness.

Margaret soon came to where the hallway ended in a

pair of white double doors gleaming in the light of her lamp. She reached out with her free hand, pulled the door open and stepped through.

She emerged into an enormous, closed arcade. The limits of its arched ceiling remained dark and indistinct twenty feet overhead as though they had not yet formed from the shadows. The light from Margaret's lamp did not reach as far as the end of the colonnade but the sounds of the approaching troop could be distinctly heard from that direction.

In a few moments, they came into view: a laughing, chattering parade of characters who had been summoned from the Umbra to take their roles and play their parts in this new Day that was just dawning here in the Tween. Huntsman, horseman, groundskeepers, maids, cooks, gentlemen in morning coats and ladies dressed to receive and be received . . . All of them came laughing and staggering out of the shadows and into existence. The great parade continued as the arcade became more real and the gas fixtures set into each column roared to life. As light filled the space, the characters in the parade suddenly gasped their approval and delight, scurrying and clambering suddenly in all directions as they scattered to populate the house.

Within moments, Margaret was standing alone on the fitted, polished tiles of the arcade floor. She held perfectly still, for she knew if the house was this solid around her then the lady of the house was drawing near.

That was when she heard it.

The shuddering breath.

The gasping for air.

"And so the new Day begins," Margaret muttered to herself. She turned toward a credenza next to the doors that she had just passed through. She set down her lamp and trimmed it down until the flame was low. She kept her hand around the back of the glass at the top and extinguished the lamp with a single puffing blow. She left the lamp there for she knew that she would have no need of it again and stepped quickly over the tiles toward the far end of the arcade. There, a staircase had appeared rising up to a second-level promenade. A plush carpet with the pattern of red roses against a black background was held firmly to the stairs with brass carpet runners. Margaret lifted the front of her skirt with both hands as she hurried up the stairs toward the sound. At the top of the stairs was a set of ornately carved oak doors richly stained and polished but Margaret did not bother with those for the sound was coming from a narrow hallway that exited from the promenade to her right.

Margaret slipped quietly into the narrow passage. It appeared to be intended for servants to move through the house, for the finish work here was far less grand than in the arcade that she had just left. The sticks of the wainscoting were painted but had a rough finish and the floor was bare wood. The hall itself jogged in mazelike angles as though it had been fitted as an afterthought around and between more important rooms. There were more doors here, each one closed, which she passed at the regular intervals and gave them no further thought, for the sounds of the labored breathing were getting more pronounced.

It was around the next corner that she found her.

Margaret's sudden appearance startled the other woman, causing her to cry out as she stumbled backward into the corner of the alcove closet.

She wore the dark green jacket and the matching skirt of a traveling suit, both of which were soaked completely through. The left sleeve of the jacket and the blouse underneath were torn and stained even darker with blood. The long skirt, too, was heavily stained on the left side. Her hair was completely undone, hanging in thick, wet strands that clung to her about her face and shoulders. She was shaking visibly and, as Margaret watched, slid down the corner of the alcove until she crouched on the floor.

"So there you are, Lady Ellis," Margaret said in a voice filled both with annoyance and relief.

"M-m-margaret? Is that you?" Ellis stammered between ragged breaths.

"And who else would I be?" Margaret replied, holding her hands together in front of her in her sternest, most disapproving manner. "You've given all the household quite a fright. Everyone has been looking for you. Wherever have you been?"

"I've been . . . running. I've been running for ever so long," Ellis replied warily.

"Running, my lady?" Margaret sniffed. "Running to where?"

"Out." Ellis said the word as though it were both obvious and puzzling. "I have to get out, Margaret, you *know* that."

"Well, there'll be plenty of time for that later," Margaret said in slightly dismissive tones. "And I'll certainly not be letting you go about in a state like that especially with the hall decorated and the guests arriving! You have to dress . . ."

"Dress?" Ellis glared up at Margaret. "Don't you understand? I have to get out of here!"

"Out of here? To where?" Margaret asked with impatience. "Truly, mistress, you have been away far too long!"

"I haven't been anywhere, Margaret," Ellis said as evenly as she could manage. "Though it hasn't been for lack of trying."

Margaret rolled her eyes and sighed. From her perspective, the house seemed to have just appeared moments ago but here Ellis looked as though she had run the legs out from under herself for quite a while. Time could be funny in the house, she thought. Maybe the house had not so much appeared around Margaret as she had appeared in it. No matter. She extended her right hand down toward the crouching, bedraggled figure shivering in the corner before her. "Come with me, my lady. We'll get you out of those wet things and into something decent and fit for company. Perhaps when you are warm and rested, you'll be able to think more clearly."

Ellis hesitated for a moment, and then reached up and took Margaret's hand.

Margaret led Ellis back down the twisting hall, smiling to herself.

They had all played this Game before.

This time, Margaret knew she could win.

2

MISTRESS OF THE HOUSE

Ellis shivered as Margaret opened the door before her. The room had an overstated opulence to it, as though a European designer had been given far too much money and far too little direction in its decor. There was an ornate fireplace fitted into the opposite wall between two tall windows. The windows were dark and Ellis could hear the rain pelting the panes before it ran in wavering sheets down the glass. A bright, cheery fire flickered in the hearth, perfectly framed by the mint-green scrollwork of the fireplace's surround. An alabaster mantel sat above the fire, with another green and gold trimmed miniature alcove above the mantel framing a clock encased in a glass dome. It reminded her of the unnerving display she had seen at Summersend, filled with dead—or nearly dead—moths. Whenever someone of her acquaintance had vanished, another moth had appeared pinned in the jar.

Ellis shivered, trying to shake the memory off.

Reaching higher still above that was a framed mirror whose arched peak nearly reached the ceiling twelve feet above the floor. Jade and marble wainscoting surrounded the room with clean, white walls. To her right she could see an enormous poster bed with a headboard and footboard of carefully polished mahogany. The coverlet appeared to be as soft and inviting as the oversized pillows that nearly obscured the headboard entirely. Ellis was not sleepy but as she stood shivering in the doorway looking at the bed, she realized that she longed for rest.

She turned to peer to her left. There was a large, ornate dressing table set against the wall, cream colored and also trimmed in gold. Set in the corner beyond near one of the windows were a pair of matching chairs and a circular claw-foot table. Each was made of the same material as the bed, its surfaces gleaming with the same finish.

One of the chairs had an ornate silk dress carefully draped over it. It was white with a diamond pattern quilted into the bodice. Large, black pom-poms adorned the front in a single line branching around along the edges of a peplum skirt at the waist. An unbelievably wide Elizabethan ruff formed the collar. On the table beyond sat a white cloche hat crowned with yet another black pompom and beside it a white-sequined mask. Gazing at the elegant costume, Ellis was suddenly conscious of how miserable she felt in the thick, soaked traveling suit she wore.

Ellis stepped cautiously into the room, her eyes fixed on the dress in the corner.

"Well, it's about time you showed your face!"

Ellis started visibly at the unexpected voice coming from the corner just inside the door. She turned, taking several steps backward into the room, her hands reflexively rising in front of her.

"Ellis, you hardly need a costume, you're such a fright already," the young woman said with a giggle. "I didn't mean to startle you."

Ellis drew in a long, shuddering breath. When she had last seen Alicia Van der Meer, she had been undeniably dead, a shriveled and shrunken corpse. Now she stood before her dressed as an Egyptian queen of the ancient world. A pattern of near-Eastern wall paintings adorned the wide hem of her long dress and the tops of her sleeves. A glittering gorgerine—a necklace of layered disks— hung around her neck while, from a circlet of gold around Alicia's head, a rearing cobra stared back at her. She was the picture of ancient royalty yet somehow Ellis could not get the image of her as the mummy she had last seen her as out of her mind. It was unnerving to see this restored woman standing before her suddenly and incredibly alive.

"Alicia?" Ellis said, blinking. "Are you all right?"

"And how else would you have me be?" Alicia replied with a mischievous grin.

Ellis threw her arms around Alicia. "I am so sorry for what happened to you!"

"Ellis, stop it!" Alicia laughed as she pushed Ellis away. "You'll ruin the dress."

"You . . . you were dead . . . both of you," Ellis stammered, blinking as though to comprehend what her eyes could not believe.

Margaret's eyes narrowed. "Is madam playing one of her tricks again? It is in poor taste for her ladyship to be jesting in such a manner."

"No, Margaret . . . Alicia . . . please," Ellis said quickly, her words coming in a rush. "I've got to find Jenny!"

"But of course you do. We *all* do," Alicia replied. "That's the whole point, isn't it? We're all looking for Jenny!"

"What?" Ellis shook her head. "No! I've got to find her and get out of here!"

"Be calm, your ladyship," Margaret said, her eyes narrowing critically. She turned toward Alicia with a critical frown. "It's that old trouble flaring up again. Perhaps you should go and fetch the doctor . . ."

"NO!" Ellis shouted, her voice demanding and firm.

Both Margaret and Alicia glared back at her.

"I mean," Ellis said carefully, "I am in no need of the doctor. I am perfectly well. I just need a little time to myself before . . . before . . ."

"The reception, madam," Margaret prompted.

"There is a reception?" *What game are these two playing at?* she thought.

"Yes, madam; before the masquerade."

"Yes, of course," Ellis said carefully. Her eyes remained fixed on Margaret. "Thank you, Margaret. You've been a great help."

Margaret hesitated, giving a glance sideways at Alicia that was not returned.

"I am sure you have other duties to attend to," Ellis said in measured words. "Alicia will attend to me. That will be all, Margaret."

"Your ladyship," Margaret protested, "it is my duty to see that you are properly dressed and prepared for this evening's—"

"I have a private matter to discuss with Miss Van der Meer," Ellis said, her voice strong and brooking no argument. "That will be all, Margaret."

"I'll . . . I'll return in half an hour, your ladyship." The woman frowned but curtsied slightly before she left the room, closing the door behind her.

Ellis took in a deep breath, her eyes shifting to Alicia.

"Miss Kendrick, it seems, had taken the liberty of choosing the costume for madam this evening," Alicia said through a pleasant, if insincere, smile. She crossed the room toward the party dress draped over the chair. She swept it up in a single motion, holding it up for Ellis's inspection as though she had taken up Margaret's role as her lady's maid. "I believe it will draw out the color in madam's eyes."

Ellis drew in a breath as she gazed at Alicia.

"Ellis," Alicia asked in a cautious voice, "what is it?"

"Alicia," Ellis said carefully. "Who are you?"

"You are in a mood tonight," the woman replied, her brows knitting slightly and her eyes narrowing as she spoke. "You know better than anyone who I am."

"No, Alicia, I mean who are you supposed to be?" Ellis glanced around the room. "What's your part in this charade they call life here?"

"I am your best friend." Alicia's lips parted slightly and she spoke through clenched teeth. "I travelled with you when you were so ill abroad. I am your companion and confidant. I am here for you, Ellis. It was your husband who brought me here to stay with you during your recovery."

"I don't have a husband," Ellis said.

"You don't *remember* a husband," Alicia said through a crooked grin. "Practically the same thing. Rather daring of you, I must say, to have a husband. It's never been done in our circles and no one is really sure what to make of the idea. But you *are* Lady Ellis after all. Who are any of them to question your behavior—especially me?"

"You hate it, don't you," Ellis said. "You hate serving me."

"We all have our part to play, Ellis." Alicia looked away and sighed, her hands running longingly down the smooth silk of the white dress in her hands.

"Alicia," Ellis said softly. "What part am I supposed to play?"

Her friend looked up sharply. "You are Lady Ellis, mistress of Echo House . . . as you have always been."

"Alicia, no!" Ellis took a step toward the woman, her eyes pleading. "I'm Ellis . . . just Ellis. You helped me try to escape Gamin. We tried to flee on the train—you, me and Ely—but the train brought us back into the town. The demon found you—killed you—and now it's the train all over again in a house that never ends. I don't want to play this terrible game anymore and I think you don't want to, either."

"This game?" Alicia burst out the words as a laugh. She carefully replaced the dress over the back of the chair. "This game is all there is. It's all there ever will be."

"That's not true," Ellis replied.

Alicia gestured to the small stool in front of the makeup table. "Will you please sit down?"

"Alicia, why are you . . ."

"Please." Alicia cocked her head slightly to the right, her voice adamant as she again made the gesture with emphasis. "Sit down."

Ellis stood looking at the immovable Alicia for an interminable time before drawing in a long breath and sitting on the stool facing the mirror. Alicia swept up a towel from off of the chair next to her and moved behind Ellis almost at once. Ellis thought it odd that the woman should be obsessed with getting her hair dry when her clothing was still so obviously soaked through.

"Look, this party is being thrown by your husband as a celebration of your return to the house," Alicia said quietly as she worked the towel about Ellis's hair. "However, having been abroad for so long a time, perhaps her ladyship has become . . . unaccustomed to the rules of polite society."

"And, I trust"—Ellis spoke the words as lightly as she could manage—"you have been instructed to guide me in these matters?"

"It should be my privilege to do so, your ladyship," Alicia continued, tossing the towel back toward the chair. She took up a long-toothed comb from the table and started the work of untangling Ellis's hair. She moved the comb carefully through Ellis's tangled locks, taking the time to gently unravel the snags. "Now that you are home, we would not want you to embarrass yourself or the house with inappropriate behavior."

"Indeed?" Ellis said, her voice quiet. "And what if I don't want to behave appropriately?"

The comb stopped in Alicia's hands. Her voice was quavering as she spoke in almost a whisper. "No, Ellis, please! They'll find out . . . *he'll* find out."

Ellis, frustrated, looked about her. There were knobs to drawers on either side of the table. She snatched at one of them, pulling on it sharply.

The table scraped against the hardwood floor with a terrible squeal.

"It's fake," Ellis said to Alicia under her breath. "Not even the drawers are real . . . they're just painted on."

"I'll ring for the handyman," Alicia said with a slightly distracted tone. "He'll have those fixed in no time."

"That's not the point!" Ellis snapped. "There's a cheery fire in the fireplace in this room but it's not giving off any heat! It's as though we are living in a doll's house."

"You didn't give him enough time," Alicia said in a rush of whispered words. "This is a very old Book and he wasn't prepared to change the Day. He's never had to build anything this quickly before. It will take him time to get the details right."

"Who? For who to get the details right?" Ellis demanded.

"The lord of the m-manor," Alicia stuttered slightly as she replied. "Your husband, of course."

"And just who is this 'husband' I'm supposed to have?" Ellis asked, both knowing and dreading the answer.

"Lord Merrick," Alicia whined, drawing back as though Ellis might strike her.

Ellis hissed her words through clenched teeth. "He set this up so that I am the lady of the house and *he* is the lord? How very convenient for him!"

"He's just trying to please you," Alicia burbled. "He's just trying to please us all."

"Please you?" Ellis was astonished at the statement. "Alicia, you more than anyone else know what is at stake. You've seen the madness of this place. You wanted to leave it as much as I. If you could only just—ouch!"

Alicia had tugged sharply on a tangle in Ellis's hair.

"Sorry," Alicia said. "That was my fault."

"Stop pretending, Alicia." Ellis pushed on in earnest, turning to face the woman. "We can do this. Together, with your help, we can find our way to the Gate."

"No, Ellis," Alicia implored. "Don't speak of it!"

"You were there," Ellis continued. "I don't remember much but I *do* remember you were there when I left. You saw what happened. We found the Gate together once and we can find it again. We can leave this place . . ."

"No!"

"Why not?" Ellis demanded.

Now it was Alicia's turn to shiver in the room. "Don't you know what happened to me after I tried to help you in Gamin? I was cast out. Out into the . . . into the Bad Place. The Nothing Place. Those were the rules, Ellis, and you made me believe I could break the rules. But I *can't*. I can't go back there again and you can't go back either."

"Why?" Ellis asked. "Why can I not go back?"

"I don't know," Alicia said simply. "It's a rule."

"Rules!" Ellis turned in exasperation away from Alicia.

"Merrick's rules! Rules he makes up that benefit only him and punish the rest of us. It's hopeless!"

Alicia stepped hesitantly back toward Ellis as she spoke. She leaned close to her ear as she whispered, her hands resting gently on Ellis's shoulders. "No, not hopeless, Ellis. There are rules that were written before Merrick; rules that cannot be changed or ignored. There must always be a Gate. Whoever's Day we are playing, somehow I know that they must obey that rule. Maybe Merrick likes to hide the Gate and maybe he's gotten quite clever at it but he cannot destroy it and he cannot keep us from it."

Ellis reached up and laid her hand on Alicia's.

Alicia considered for a moment. "The soldiers know about the Gate and so does Dr. Carmichael. Maybe that friend of yours . . ."

"Jonas?" Ellis said, her voice flat as she spoke the name.

"Yes." Alicia stepped again behind Ellis and, hesitantly at first, began again to untangle her hair.

"I don't know who Jonas is," Ellis replied. "At least, not yet. I know who he *says* he is, but I don't trust him any more than I trust Merrick."

"It's your funeral, Ellis."

Ellis considered for a moment. She still did not remember who she was or from where she had come. She was not even sure whether she was alive or dead. All she had were the words of others telling her who she was and those from people she no longer trusted.

You can't win the game until you know the rules . . .

Ellis closed her eyes. It was a memory from long ago. It sounded in her mind like a woman's voice but there was no name or face or place associated with it.

You have to learn the rules before you can break them . . .

Another voice in her memory and this time a man's voice. A voice that made her smile. She tried desperately to hang on to the memory but it was gone as a wave retreating from the shore. Nothing more.

"Alicia, just when is this masquerade?" Ellis asked.

"Within the hour, I believe," she replied.

"Indeed." Ellis nodded. Ellis eyed the costume dress still draped over the chair. "You say I've been mistress of this house before?"

"I don't believe there were any others before you," Alicia said more cheerfully.

"Was I a good mistress?"

The strokes of the comb through Ellis's hair hesitated for a moment before continuing.

Ellis considered for a moment and then rephrased her question. "Perhaps what I meant to ask was, 'Was I good at playing the part of the mistress?'"

"You were always the best in your Day," Alicia replied.

You have to learn the rules before you can break them.

"Thank you, Alicia," Ellis sighed. "Let me rest for a few minutes and then come back with Margaret to help me dress."

"Of course, dearest friend," Alicia replied.

Ellis turned toward the window. She could not see

through the sheets of rain pelting the glass to anything that may be in the darkness beyond. "I guess the weather will prevent us from going outside."

"Outside?" Alicia giggled. "What a fanciful notion! May I be of any further service, Ellis?"

"Not now," Ellis said with a smile playing at the edges of her lips. "But perhaps later."

3

MASQUERADE

Ellis set her jaw and started up the stairs. The treads were covered in a deep pile, crimson carpet held firmly in place by bright brass carpet runners. The mahogany railings on both sides were ornately carved and polished to a gleaming shine. The newel posts at the top of the railings each supported a golden candelabra, each of which was fitted with a plethora of small electric bulbs that filled the space with bright illumination. At the top of the stairs was a landing, the back wall of which was composed almost entirely of a stained glass window that rose nearly fifteen feet to the coffered ceiling overhead. It was a bright and inviting space that seemed to gently beckon her toward the upper rooms.

Ellis took every step with dread.

She wore the costume that Margaret had laid out for

her. Despite Alicia's repeated assurances that Ellis had chosen the costume herself, she had no memory of doing so.

Ellis hesitated on the stairs and smiled grimly to herself. It would not have been the first thing that she had
forgotten. Indeed, it seemed far more likely that she would
have no memory of something than that she should recall it. Nevertheless, she felt certain that this would not
have been a costume that she would have chosen for
herself. The outfit was perfectly tailored to her form but
there was something about this costume in particular—a
black-on-white rendition of a clown—that she found
distasteful and slightly obscene. But her own clothing was
soaked and this was the only option that presented itself.

Besides, she reminded herself, if one were to learn the
rules of the game, one had to play the part.

"Ellis, are you all right?" Alicia, only a step or two
behind her and slightly to her left, reached forward and
took Ellis's elbow in her hand as though to steady her.

Ellis turned and smiled at Alicia, conveying a gentle
humor that she did not feel. "Quite all right. Perhaps just
a little overexcited."

Alicia, resplendent in her Egyptian accoutrements,
smiled sweetly back at her in reply.

I wonder if she is lying to me as much as I am lying to her,
Ellis thought as she turned and continued up the staircase.

Her eyes became fixed for a moment on the stained
glass window. It was a beautiful design with an intricate,
high level of detail. It was a curious depiction and yet

somehow familiar. There were two figures: one each of a man and a woman. The man was shown wearing a powder-blue morning coat and pants while the woman was in a long gown of a matching color. They stood side by side with their arms extended slightly from their bodies, their palms facing outward. From their open hands, great swirling patterns of glass and color flowed, spiraling outward, forming patterns on either side of them that when taken together reminded Ellis of the wings of a lunar moth. As she reached the landing she could make out minute details embedded in the glass more clearly: ruins, castle towers, forests, jungles, desert dunes, schooners, along with buildings and towns of every era and description. One in particular caught her eye. It looked almost exactly like the home that she had occupied in Gamin with her cousin, Jenny, before the world had gone mad. Ellis leaned in closer as she thought she had seen figures moving in the glass depiction of her seaside home.

"Ellis, please hurry," Alicia urged. "Everyone is waiting for you."

Ellis turned reluctantly away from the stained glass. The landing led to a pair of staircases on either side that doubled back to either side of a balustrade that overlooked the stairwell. Ellis could hear the loud clatter of her heels against the stone treads echoing about the stairwell. There seemed otherwise to be a terrible silence, as though the house itself were holding its breath.

At the top of the stairs was a set of double doors with

frosted glass into a pattern of leaded panes. Beyond the glass, shadows shifted back and forth.

Ellis hesitated.

"What is it now?" Alicia demanded.

For a moment, Ellis wished that she were back in Gamin. There, at least, the world largely made sense. She knew little more now about herself than she did when she had first arrived at that train station. But at least in that seaside town she had some hope of normality. Now, however, she was in a world where she could trust nothing and no one.

You have to know the rules before you can win the game . . .

She furrowed her brow and then stepped resolutely toward the doors. She grasped both handles, turned them and pulled.

The sudden cheer startled her.

The room beyond was crowded in the extreme, packed tightly with costumed revelers from blue wall to blue wall. All of them turned the caricatures of their masked faces toward Ellis, each adding their voice to the tumult that struck her like an unexpected wave on the shore. She was confronted in that moment by a dizzying array of costumes and false faces. The woman whose gown was that of a shepherdess but whose mask resembled the visage of a lamb. A samurai wearing a grinning Kabuki mask. A figure in pantaloons covered entirely in pinfeathers with the hood that obscured their face in the shape of an owl's head extending down into a cape resembling wings. The strange menagerie poured out through the double doors, chattering, screeching and burbling as they surrounded and engulfed Ellis.

"It's all for you, Ellis," beamed Alicia. She took Ellis by her arm, drawing her into the blue room. "He did it all for you."

The crowd surged around her. The room was far too small for this number of people. Ellis felt the stifling closeness and a rising panic within her. Between the masked faces, overly elaborate headpieces, farcical hats and hairdos, she glimpsed open doorways that led to further rooms that seemed to be just as crowded and claustrophobic as the one she was in.

Ellis turned, searching for the door through which they had just entered, but she was having difficulty seeing it through the press of people. She felt dizzy, disoriented, and her breaths were coming quickly. She closed her eyes, trying to push away the confusion and overwhelming colors surrounding her. Then, as if at her will, everything stilled.

"Welcome home, Ellis."

Ellis's eyes flew open, her head jerking toward the sound.

"Merrick," she said, her tone as much accusation as recognition.

Merrick stood before her, beaming at her with a toothy, brilliant smile. His costume struck Ellis as that of a jester: a carefully fitted jacket with narrow matching pants, both of which displayed a symmetrical pattern of rectangles each made up of two opposing red triangles with green and blue triangles filling out the remaining sides. His gleaming white shoes were topped by ridiculously large balls made of the same material. Like Ellis, he, too, sported a ruff around his collar, although his was much smaller than hers. In his right hand he held an elaborate mask comprised of the features of three faces, each sharing the eye socket with the face to either side. In his left hand, he held a club-like object composed of two wooden slats bound tightly together at one end. Ellis took all of this in quickly and moved on in her mind. She knew that this plumage was just camouflage, bright colors and patterns meant to distract her.

She concentrated instead on his face. It was a visage that she had come to know well since her arrival in Gamin. It was a painfully handsome face. His jawline had sharp and soft angles at once, obscured by the shadow of his heavy beard, which no amount of careful shaving could completely eradicate. He had a slightly aquiline nose that put Michelangelo's *David* to shame. His unfashionably long hair was coiffed in a way that might have suggested a nonchalance to his appearance had he not so obviously taken such care in creating its look.

Yet it was his eyes that finally caught her, as they always did. They were a striking light blue that even in his apparent current ferment held a hint of sadness and confusion. There was anticipation there, too, she thought, and she wondered for a moment if these were the same eyes the mouse looked into just before the cobra struck.

In an instant, however, his countenance changed. His eyes became downcast, his brow troubled and his shoulders slightly bowed.

"Yes, Ellis, it is me," Merrick said in penitent tones. "And I fear that I have given you reason for pain in hearing my name."

A sigh of sympathy came from the masked faces crowding the room about them.

"I was terribly concerned for you when you returned," he continued, his gaze rising from the floor to gauge her reaction. "Down all the ages of our existence, no one had ever left. I had hoped to make your return easier, to create for you a space where perhaps you could gradually regain yourself."

"Is that what Gamin was all about?" Ellis said, her mouth dry at saying the words.

"Mistakes were made." Merrick nodded. "I'll grant you that."

"Friends vanishing without a trace? Mass murder? Demonic monsters in the street?" Ellis's eyes remained fixed on Merrick. "These were 'mistakes'?"

The masks uttered an audible gasp.

"It was Dr. Carmichael," Merrick replied after a moment's hesitation. He straightened up, the old assurance that she always found suspicious reasserting itself. "I should've never taken his advice. Those manifestations were entirely his doing. I realize now that he never had your best interests at heart. But now that that terrible nightmare is over, I can properly welcome you home back among the friends and acquaintances who have so longed for your return—"

"And where is Jenny?" Ellis demanded.

"Jenny?" Merrick appeared annoyed that his speech had been interrupted.

"Yes, my cousin Jenny," Ellis reiterated, her voice stronger and more insistent.

Merrick once again beamed a great smile and then began to laugh heartily. His arms opened wide as he gestured with a mask in one hand and the slapstick in the other, pivoting as though to encompass the entire company of grotesque masked revelers.

"Why, Jenny *is* the game," Merrick exclaimed. "We shall have a treasure hunt throughout the house! You all know Jenny March, Ellis's cousin. She is our houseguest and the game is that she must be found."

Squeals of delight mingled with the murmur of excitement, and a smattering of clapping rippled from room to room among the partiers.

Ellis spoke to Merrick through clenched teeth. "Where is she?"

Merrick was nearly a full head taller than her, looking down at her in puzzlement. "But that's the whole point of the game. Finding Jenny."

"You've hidden her somewhere," Ellis said. She could

feel the heat of her anger rising in her face. "Tell me where she is!"

"I did no such thing!" Merrick seemed insulted at the suggestion. "She hid herself. It would be such a terrible game otherwise."

"Ellis," Alicia said, her hand touching Ellis's elbow. "It really should be a very good game. Don't you think we could play? Perhaps, just for a little while?"

"Everyone, please, I shall need your attention for a moment," Merrick said, his voice booming over the murmuring of the crowd. "To begin the game, I have secured the assistance of the Nightbirds Society in preparing a theatrical offering, the libretto of which may assist you in your quest."

The excited response of the revelers threatened for a moment to overwhelm Merrick's oration. He held up his hands to quiet the crowd once more.

"Let us all move quickly into the theater," Merrick roared, "and let the comedy begin!"

Merrick swung around to Ellis's left, his right hand closing on her upper arm in a viselike grip. On her right, Alicia had locked her arm through Ellis's. Both of them at once began drawing Ellis through the crowd past the doorway into the green room and toward the orange room beyond. The laughing and excited masked figures around her were moving in that direction, too, forming an inexorable river of flesh and propelling her forward.

Ellis swallowed hard. The crush of the masked costumes

around her made her want to scream but she was determined to learn the rules of the game that everyone else
was playing. She glanced at Merrick, trying to ask a
question as casually as she could. "What is this comedy
about?"

Merrick gave a lopsided grin. "Truth, Ellis. Truth and
the past."

Three sets of double doors were open on the far side
of the orange room. The crowd was pouring through
them into the darkness of the theater beyond.

Ellis forced herself to take a deep breath. "And who is
the principal character in this farce?"

Merrick bared his teeth again. "Why, you are, of
course!"

4

SHADOW PLAY

*A*s Ellis was ushered through the theater doors, the gaslights along the walls burst into light, illuminating the room. It was a dreadfully small space for a theater. There were only eight chairs across in each row with no center aisle. Indeed, she half expected there to be pews rather than the chairs, for the space reminded her more of a private chapel on an estate than a proper theater, despite the slanting angle of the floor toward the stage. Fresco panels adorned the arched ceiling depicting characters wearing both tragic and comedic masks in what appeared to be unsettling scenes. One depicted a child in the crib fitted with a mask of a wailing baby while a pair of figures in elegant costumes and masked as crows leaned over the child. Another showed a gate, overgrown with vines, brush and trees to the point of it being nearly completely obscured. A third showed a comically small sailing ship tossed in a storm with the four hapless members of its crew all staring back at her through tragic masks. This last particularly caught her attention as she could make out the smallest figure of a lighthouse far in the background of the image. The edges of each fresco were heavily gilded in gold leaf or possibly paint. The stage at the front was narrow and tall, an arched proscenium filled entirely by a lush, red velvet curtain. The slight, bold thrust of the stage in front of the curtain was rimmed with footlights that illuminated the curtain. A matching set of short stairs gave access to the front of the stage from the aisles on either side of the main floor. There was a small balcony in the back that had already filled in its few seats with the costumed and masked audience. Still others in the balcony stood at its edges and crowded the exits. The revelers from the masquerade who rushed onto the main floor moved down either side, laughing and chattering as they, too, rushed for the few available seats. Despite the press, three chairs remained vacant in the center of the front row. It was toward these that Merrick and Alicia quickly guided Ellis.

"Isn't this wondrous, Ellis?" Alicia beamed as she guided Ellis toward the center open seat in the front row.

"That would be one word for it," Ellis responded, licking her lips.

"We spared nothing in preparing this for you, Ellis,"

Merrick said. "This is our gift to you for all you've done for us."

Ellis merely smiled politely as she sat down, the clown costume rustling slightly. She reminded herself to keep breathing.

A figure in the caricature of a French officer's uniform strutted onto the stage from the wings. He wore an oversized bicorne hat and a smiling mask of pallid blue with red streaks coming from the eye sockets that gave the appearance of blood. As he came to center stage, he faced the audience. He reached up with his right hand, removing the mask with a flourish.

"I know him," Ellis murmured to herself. Silenus Tune had been one of the people she had meet in Gamin. Only slightly taller than herself, he had a young, clean-shaven face with a mischievous, one-sided cant to his smile that always put her on her guard.

"Lord Merrick and Lady Ellis," Silenus said, bowing deeply toward them both in the front row. He then gave a less gracious bow to the rest of the audience. "And to everyone else of far lesser consequence! The Nightbirds Society is pleased to present . . ."

Ellis braced herself. The Nightbirds Literary Society had been Jenny's social club in Gamin. That it should exist in this house of eternal horrors as well was both significant and disturbing.

"The Tragedy of Jenny March!"

Ellis's gasp was covered completely by the roar of approval from the audience.

"Oh, a tragedy!" Alicia beamed, clapping her hands together lightly. "Those are the best. Ever so much more engaging."

"Let the play begin!" Merrick called out.

The great velvet curtain rose behind Silenus as he bowed deeply a second time. The stage was bare behind him, the raw bricks of the back wall exposed and only a pair of tormentors to frame the sides of the proscenium.

"If we take you back, dear friends. Back before the beginning." Silenus took several steps backward toward the center of the exposed stage as he spoke. "For in that time there was a king; a king of light and darkness, of hot and cold, of vengeance and forgiveness."

Silenus beckoned with his left hand for someone to come out of the wings. A costumed figure that was entirely yellow on one side and purple on the other strutted onto the stage and began striking poses for the audience as Silenus continued his narration.

"The king was the embodiment of contradiction," Silenus continued as he seemed to conduct the actor onstage through his performance. "His head yearned for reason but his heart argued against it. His hands yearned to stay and create but his feet longed to wander. He knew that he must choose between the two halves of his contradiction but could not do so on his own and so he called together his great, large family that they might all advise him as to what to do."

Silenus then pointed to a number of the revelers who were standing in both the aisles. With a flick of his hand, he gestured for them to come up on stage and take their places in the drama.

"Among them were two brothers," Silenus offered as the excited people he had beckoned onstage settled down. As he spoke the words, one man in a costume that resembled a dragon gently pushed his way through the crowd to stand at the front of the stage. Another man in a costume that resembled a pale horse did likewise from the opposite side. "One of the brothers was the champion of order, obedience and law. The second brother argued for choice, discovery and freedom. They fell to quarreling and soon all of their brothers and sisters were being asked to choose between one side and the other, one brother against the other. It was in this time, with the rumbling thunders of contention threatening war, that all of the host—even good friends—were broken by the streams of choice."

"Oh, isn't it wonderful!" Alicia said. "I just love this part."

Ellis continued to watch the stage. There were now four or five main characters at the forefront of the stage, Silenus being one, and some sort of battle going on in the background between the two sides. One of the main characters, dressed as a vagabond, appeared to side with

the group on the right side of the stage while two characters in peacock costumes set a gate on the stage between
the two warring sides and the other main characters fled
through it. The character in the vagabond costume
attempted to follow but was unable to pass through. They
then crouched next to the gate apparently hiding in wait.

"It is a very old story," said Merrick, his eyes fixed on
Ellis rather than the stage. "Do you not remember it,
Ellis? Is it not familiar to you?"

"No, Merrick," Ellis finally replied. "I cannot make
heads or tails of it. What has any of this got to do with
Jenny?"

Anger flashed in Merrick's eyes as his face flushed and
he jumped up, facing the stage.

"Second act!" Merrick shouted at the actors onstage.

Silenus stammered for a moment in the middle of his
oration and then stopped. He quickly ushered everyone
off stage and hurried his extras back down the stairs and
into the aisles once more.

"Well, this is moving along rather quickly," said Alicia,
shrugging.

"Uh, second act? Yes, of course." Silenus gnawed at
his lip for a moment in thought and then held up his
beckoning hand toward the center of the front row. "Lady
Ellis, may we impose upon you? We shall certainly need
you for this act."

Ellis felt a chill run down the center of her back. "Oh,
no. I couldn't possibly . . ."

"But you must, my dear," Merrick said. "It is the *commedia dell'arte* and, after all, an important part of the Game."

"Oh, go on, Ellis," Alicia urged. "It's only a play."

"You do want to find Jenny, don't you?" Merrick's face was blank, his eyebrows raised.

Ellis drew in a breath and stood up. She made her way around to the left side of the stage and started up the stairs. The packed theater erupted in applause and cheers. She followed the directions of Silenus and stood facing the audience in the center of the stage. The vista in front of her made her shiver. All of the bizarre and garish masks and costumes staring back at her made her wonder for a moment if the actors were in the audience and the audience was onstage.

"Oh, tragedy indeed!" said Silenus as he frowned and wiped away unseen tears from his mask. "But then again, what is the second act for if it is not for competition, heartache and inexplicable sorrow. Pain, indeed, thy name is second act!"

Margaret, as if on cue, stepped onto the stage from the shadowy distance of the wings. She was not in costume but was still in her plain black dress, her hair bundled tightly at the back of her head. When she spoke, however, her voice had a strange accent to it. "Miss Ellis, you in fo' a whoopin' now. I'z don' know what yo mamma's gonna do."

Ellis gaped at Margaret. She shook her head, uncertain what to do.

Silenus slipped quietly up behind her and prompted Ellis by whispering in her ear. "Say '*She doesn't have to know.*'"

"She doesn't have to know," repeated Ellis.

The audience drew in a collective breath.

"Oh, yez she does," Margaret continued near her on the barren stage. "Ain't no way you gonna keep this a secret any longer. How you managed this long is beyond me!"

The pair of peacocks entered again from the side of the stage that was behind her. They brought in with them a tall set of doors, which they held upright between Ellis and the back of the stage.

Silenus whispered again in Ellis's ear. *"Even if she knows . . ."*

"Even if she knows . . ." Ellis said aloud.

"It doesn't change a thing," Silenus continued.

"It doesn't change a thing."

"You had best to stay out of this," Silenus murmured.

"You had best to stay out of this, Emma," Ellis said.

Margaret opened her mouth to speak, only it was no longer Margaret. A thin, hunched-over black woman in a servant's dress had taken her place on the stage.

"It's your funeral," the black woman said.

The audience behind Ellis roared with laughter.

Ellis gaped at the woman in the servant's dress. "Your name . . . Your name is Emma."

"Yes, Miss Ellis," the woman replied with a puzzled look of her own. "You've known me since you drew your first breath. What kind of game are you playing at now, child?"

"Ellis!"

It was another voice, this time from the back of the stage. In the moment the two peacocks pulled aside the doors and vanished with them into the wings.

There, toward the back of stage, was a woman in an elegant purple dress, her back as straight as that of the wingback chair in which she sat. Her hands were folded in her lap with study the precision. Her face, in its day, might have been considered to be an exceptional beauty if it had not been for a slight overbite and a minor irregularity in the straightness of her teeth. Her face was narrow, with high cheekbones. Her hair was carefully styled, a predominantly dark color partly due to the woman paying excessive attention to keeping the gray roots at bay. It was in her large, dark eyes, however, where her most formidable weapon lay and the all-too-familiar gaze with which she now fixed Ellis.

"Ellis, I have just entertained Mrs. Lawrence," the woman said without preamble. "And she has given me a report of the most alarming nature regarding your conduct. I have warned you about this time and time again and still you insist on ignoring my wishes and my direction in this. Is it true what Mrs. Lawrence has told me? Is it true what the entire street not to mention every member of our social circle and a good many beyond will be gossiping about before the sun has a chance to go down?"

A murmur of concern washed over the stage as it was uttered by the audience collectively.

Ellis started shaking, her eyes fixed on the woman in the chair.

"Are you going to answer me?"

Silenus moved to prompt her, but Ellis spoke on her own.

"Yes, Mother," she replied.

5

UNWARRANTED ACTS

*Y*es it is true or yes you're going to answer me?" the woman seated in the wingback chair demanded, although there was a quiver in her voice.

"Both, I suppose." Ellis spoke the words as though she were delivering lines in the play. They were words that she had spoken before and though it pained her to repeat them, she felt compelled to reproduce them now. It was her first and tenuous connection with the true memory of her past and yet the crushing pain of it was nearly too much to bear.

Men and women costumed as suns, moons and stars brought in a pair of painted flats that resembled her mother's drawing room of the house. One of the painted flats featured a large window. As Ellis watched, the window in the painting began to brighten with the light of an afternoon sun. Leaves on the painted trees began to move in an afternoon breeze while the muted sound of their rustling passed across the stage. Ellis could smell the lacquer of the finished wood below the wainscot of the walls.

"This is no time for your impertinence," her mother snapped at her.

Victoria Bradlee-Harkington, Ellis realized with a shock. *My mother's name.*

Victoria was not a woman to be trifled with but there was definitely pain behind her stern eyes. "This is a serious matter, young lady!"

The audience behind Ellis uttered a collective "ooh," anticipating Ellis's response.

"I quite agree," Ellis said hesitantly, drawing the words from reluctant memory. She had a terrible feeling of foreboding. *I don't want to be here. I don't want to do this again.* Yet Ellis could not help but utter the words she knew she would later regret. "I think it very serious that Mrs. Lawrence's daughter should be so shockingly unfamiliar with how humans reproduce."

The audience behind her gave an appreciative laugh. Ellis winced.

"I will not discuss such a thing here!" her mother exclaimed. "And you should have more sense than to acquaint that innocent young girl with such personal matters!"

"Well someone needed to tell her, Mother." The words came from Ellis's mouth but tears stung her eyes. "She's nearly seventeen and Sarah knew I was studying at the School of Medicine and she didn't feel comfortable asking her mother about it. That Sargent boy has been fluttering around her and from what I hear he has something of a reputation . . ."

The audience in the theater laughed out loud at the cleverness of Ellis's dialogue. She turned around in anguish.

"Stop it, Merrick!" Ellis demanded. "Make it stop!"

The masked revelers in the packed audience roared with delight.

"But that's not possible." Merrick smiled back in satisfaction. "It's *your* play! If you want to end it, then go ahead and *finish it*!"

Ellis turned to face her mother, knowing what would follow and dreading it.

"Then it *is* true," her mother said, fire in her eyes and her brow furrowed in distress. "You discussed the most intimate knowledge between a husband and a wife with Sarah Lawrence? How could you, Ellis! Her father is a bishop!"

"It's hardly a secret, Mother!" Ellis said, tears welling up in her eyes despite the hotness of her words. *Finish it!* "I'm told that people come into the world pretty much the same way everywhere. Any farm girl in the world who has ever raised so much as a dog or a pig knows more about sex than the debutantes of the Boston Brahmins."

Victoria sprang up from her chair with a suddenness

that surprised Ellis. Her mother raised her hand and brought it sharply across Ellis's face with a stinging crack.

Ellis, still wearing her clown costume, fell to the floor from the shock of the blow, just as she had remembered it. She still felt the sting of it on her hot cheek.

Victoria stood over her, trying to rub the pain from her hand. Tears were running down her cheeks as well but her mother had set her mind to a course of action and there would be no going back.

"You think this is some sort of lark?" Her mother's voice shook with her rage. "You've squandered every social opportunity we have afforded you. You've taken no interest in any of the boys we've arranged for you to meet and your behavior at your cotillion was an embarrassment to the family!"

"I am not an embarrassment!" Ellis responded on cue, though she knew that in her mother's eyes she most certainly was a heartbreaking disappointment.

"Do you know why I agreed to send you to medical school?" Victoria continued. "It was not because you idolize your father, although that is certainly true enough. I permitted it because I despaired of you ever managing to make a proper place in Boston society. I thought if you got this ridiculous notion out of your head that you might come to your senses and make a marriage that would secure your future and that of your family."

"Ah!" the audience sighed behind her, but Ellis barely heard it.

Victoria looked down on the quaking form of her daughter. She reached down toward her but then hesitated and withdrew. "I see now that this is all just a game to you, something for your mother to play at. Well, you can't win the game until you learn the rules . . ."

Ellis looked up in shock.

"The rules of Boston society are complicated and unforgiving. Their rules are my rules and now they are your rules as well," Victoria said as she slowly sat back down, regaining her cool poise as she did. "You are going to play by those rules, Ellis, or—as it is the only thing that seems to motivate you—I will take away your schooling and your ambitions after your father's profession. You have been a disappointment all my life, Ellis. I will not permit you to disappoint us again."

"Yes, Mother," Ellis the clown whimpered as she sat beaten upon the floor.

"I have arranged for you to meet that young Cabot boy," Victoria said, her voice weary and tired. "Friday at one thirty sharp at the Union Oyster House down in the North End. I understand he insists on punctuality. Do you understand, Ellis?"

"Yes, Mother."

She had understood. There would be no going back. There would never be a going back. Although she had no specific recollection, Ellis knew that things would never be the same between her and her mother after that day. While she knew nothing about their relationship before that scene nor had any memory of events afterward, she felt the deep, aching loss of the moment, the sadness that would color her thoughts of Victoria in more somber hues thereafter.

"Bravo!" cried Merrick.

Merrick's voice drew Ellis's focus from the memory playing both in her mind and on the stage. Two worlds had collided as this moment plunged into the memory of another life and back again.

In a flash of insight she looked out over the audience and whispered, "My life, I remember my real life."

The audience erupted in laughter and applause.

This world, the Tween, came sharply into focus for Ellis. She had been here before and she had left it through the Gate to somewhere beyond. She had lived the life she was seeing on the stage.

How? Why am I here again? she wondered. *Where is the stage life . . . my real life?*

Memory failed beyond the moment and the sting on her cheek felt very real. The sun, moon and stars costumes again pranced onto the stage as the applause continued. Ellis raised her tear-streaked face toward the wingback chair.

Her mother was not there. Behind the chair the painted flats were once again only paintings. Margaret was walking off the stage. Next to her, Silenus was breaking into more exposition.

"Ah, but what of this Cabot?" he said, waving his mask

with a flourish. "What of her meeting with that sad and much besotted youth?"

The previous flats were being replaced by new ones depicting an old restaurant interior, but Ellis barely knew it.

Her costume made sense to her now. She was dressed for the *commedia dell'arte*. She was the Columbine character, the "fatal woman" who was the betrayer of true love for the riches of the world. Merrick was obviously Harlequin—the trickster and seducer of Columbine.

Yet she had remembered something of her life before Gamin, before the madness and the nightmare from which she could not awaken. What did all this have to do with finding Jenny?

"Here is the restaurant, and, yes, Ellis is *late!*"

The audience cooed in anticipation.

A new character walked onto the stage from the wings. He wore a costume in white, with wide pants and puffed sleeves. His volto mask was that of a sad clown, also white with a light blue domino painted onto it in the shape of a paisley.

Pierrot, Ellis thought. *The sad clown that Columbine betrayed.* She stood up, wondering what her next lines were supposed to be.

Silenus stepped up behind her once more and whispered into her ear, "Say, 'I am sorry I am so late.'"

Ellis sighed and then repeated without enthusiasm, "I am sorry I am so late."

"Yes, it is, and it has, for me, just gotten much better," the clown said.

The clown's response was wrong and made no sense. Silenus hesitated, uncertain. He shot a glance at Merrick but got only a deep frown for direction.

The clown leaned in toward Ellis and whispered, "Begin again with, 'Good day, sir.'"

Ellis furrowed her brow, not understanding.

"Say, 'Good day, sir,'" the clown urged.

Ellis complied out of curiosity. "Good day, sir."

"Yes, it is, and it has, for me, just gotten much better," the clown responded again. "How may I help you?"

Ellis caught her breath.

The clown urged her quietly again. "Is it your watch?"

"It is my watch," Ellis said, the words rising from somewhere inside her once more. "I think . . . I think it is broken."

"Then it is fortunate that you have found me," the clown replied. "Although I'm afraid that I would prefer time to run a little slower while you're here."

A confused murmur ran through the audience behind her.

"Are you that poor of a watchmaker?" Ellis said, a smile coming to her lips at the warmth of the memory. "Or are you saying my face would stop a clock?"

The colors of the flats in the background were shifting, running together and separating. They no longer depicted a restaurant but rather the interior of a shop. Numerous clocks began emerging from the paint as though to cover the walls. The sound of their ticking quietly settled on the stage.

"Neither, miss," the clown answered with a bow. "I am just grateful for whatever time we have. You mentioned your watch?"

"Yes," Ellis replied, only mildly surprised to find a watch in her hands as she held it out. "I am in rather a hurry. I have an appointment across town and the gentleman is something of a stickler for being on time."

"Well, if I were him," the clown said from behind his mask, "then I would wait however long it pleased you."

"The watch?" Ellis insisted.

"Yes, the watch," the clown said, taking the broken timepiece. "Let me take a look."

"Have we met before?" Ellis delivered the words as she had spoken them before in this shop.

"I am sure I would have remembered you," the clown answered.

The murmur running through the audience was getting louder. Merrick stood up in the front of the theater. "What is this?"

"Sorry, of course you're right," Ellis continued, repeating the words as they came to her. "People are always saying that to each other."

"It doesn't mean they're wrong." The clown nodded. "We're meeting now and that's a good start. Your watch has a broken balance wheel, Miss . . . ?"

"Ellis." She smiled at the memory. "Ellis Harkington."

"This may take some time, Ellis," the clown said with a catch in his voice.

"There is no rush," Ellis sighed. The words she had spoken before but now there was a warmth to them that she did not understand but felt deeply. She stepped forward, breaking out of the memory. The paintings on the background flats rearranged themselves back into the depiction of a restaurant interior and fell backward onto the stage with a bang.

"I *knew* you," Ellis said. "You were there . . . I knew you in Boston! You're . . ."

"JONAS!" Merrick shouted, rushing toward the stage. "The play is finished! Let the hunt begin!"

A cheer rang out from the audience as they leaped to their feet.

Jonas grabbed Ellis's hand. "Run, Ellis! RUN!"

He pulled her toward the wings of the stage.

They ran.

6

BELOW STAIRS

Ellis trailed behind Jonas, his grip on her hand as firm as steel and, to her touch, just as cold. She caught a glimpse of the astonished face of Margaret as they slipped past her. The fire-safe stage door was wedged slightly ajar. Jonas made a beeline toward it, shoving it open with his free arm. The door swung violently open, rebounding off of the wall behind it. Ellis slipped through the opening just before the door slammed closed behind them.

Jonas did not hesitate. He turned at once to the left down a long, whitewashed hallway with mounted pipes running along the ceiling. Caged light fixtures with bare bulbs cast stark light in pools down the short length of the narrow hall that ended in a T intersection of even narrower passages. Jonas chose the right, smashing against the wall as he careened around the corner. Ellis, too, crashed against the wall but was dragged forward again almost at once by Jonas's unrelenting grip.

"Where are you taking me?" Ellis asked, her breath already coming in short gulps.

"Away," Jonas replied. His volto mask still clung to his face. "As far away as possible."

"But *where*," she demanded.

"Anywhere!" Jonas cried out.

Their costumes rubbed against the narrowing walls. Ellis could see a wooden door at the end of the passage but the walls seemed to be closing in on them. She wondered for a moment if they would become stuck before they reached the door.

Voices echoed from the corridor behind them. Laughing voices. Giggling voices. Hysterical, disparate and desperate voices.

Jonas snatched at the latch handle. It shifted reluctantly and, in a moment, the wooden door swung open onto darkness.

Ellis cried out as Jonas pulled her in with him.

Jonas pressed the door closed behind them. Ellis's eyes quickly grew accustomed to the dim light. They stood on a landing of an open stairwell. The stairs were narrow, made of wood with an oil finish. She looked up but could not make out the ceiling let alone the top landing of the stairs. She leaned forward slightly against the railing to look downward. It gave slightly at her touch. She pulled back but even in that moment knew that she could not perceive the bottom of the stairwell, either.

"Don't stop, Ellis," Jonas whispered urgently to her. "We have to keep going."

"Going?" Ellis gaped. "I'm not going anywhere until you—"

"Stop it!" Jonas demanded, his voice firm, as though he would brook no opposition. "For this once, Ellis, just listen to me. Don't argue. Don't question. Don't doubt. Just follow me. Can you do that for just a few minutes until we're somewhere safe?"

Ellis felt her face redden. She wanted to defy him . . . was shocked at how natural it felt to defy him . . .

The muted murmur of voices could be heard on the other side of the door.

Ellis held her tongue and only nodded.

Jonas drew in a deep breath and then plunged down the stairs with Ellis in tow. They traversed several flights, each time coming to a landing with a door identical to the door they had just left on the previous landing. Jonas, however, did not appear to be looking at the exits at all, but rather was counting to himself with each landing to which they descended. Finally he muttered, "Seven!" to himself, reached out for the doorknob and pulled open the door.

He ran almost at once into the metal frame of a small bed that nearly filled the bare room. The steel legs screeched horribly as the frame scraped across the floor. Jonas swore indistinctly through teeth clenched against the pain, and pulled Ellis around the bed toward the door on the opposite side.

It was a nursery. The room was ornately decorated in muted Alice blue and light pink tones. There was a coffered ceiling in this room with a rocking chair set near an unlit fireplace and a large bassinet in the corner.

The wailing of a baby's lusty cries were coming from the bassinet.

"Wait!" Ellis cried out. "The baby . . ."

"Not now, Ellis," Jonas insisted, pulling her across the room by the viselike grip of his hand.

"There's no one here to take care of it," Ellis protested. "We have to do something . . ."

"There is nothing we can do for it." Jonas scowled, his brow knitted in determination. "Not for it or for anyone else here."

"So, we're just leaving this child?" Ellis was aghast.

"It doesn't matter," Jonas said, impatience coloring his words. "Come on!"

The door should have led to a closet but instead opened onto a steep, narrow staircase plunging downward. At the base of the stairs more than twenty feet below them, dim bulbs cast an amber light from wall-mounted iron sconces set on either side of a door with peeling, beige paint.

Jonas stepped onto the stairs carefully. He glanced backward at Ellis, his free hand raising a finger to his lips, begging her to be quiet as well. The stairs creaked softly beneath their feet as they descended. At the next door, Jonas paused, listening for any sound on the other side. Satisfied, he turned the tarnished brass handle and pushed it open.

Ellis stepped through into a broad hallway. It had a floor of fitted tiles that shone in the incandescent glow from punch-bowl lights mounted to the ceiling at even intervals. There was a bench set to one side of the hall between a pair of closed doors finished in white paint. Across from these was a matching set of open doorframes. Through them Ellis caught a glimpse of a pristine kitchen unsullied by a dirty dish or cooking sauce. It was strange, Ellis thought, that nothing was happening in the one room in the house that she knew should be busy nearly every moment of a waking day.

I know you think you have to learn these things, but you upset Cook whenever she finds you in her kitchen.

Ellis's hand went to her head. That voice. Her mother's voice.

Cook is doing something every moment of the day in her domain and she has no time to take you on as an apprentice as well.

"Ellis," Jonas said, carefully examining her face. "Are you all right?"

"Yes, I am fine," Ellis snapped, stepping back and snatching her hand sharply away from his entwining fingers. "But, you . . . I *remember* you."

Jonas gave her a smile that was colored by the pain in his eyes. "Yes, I very much hope you do."

"Don't be too certain that's a good thing," Ellis insisted, keeping her distance. "I'm not. Take off that mask."

Jonas drew in a breath.

"Now," Ellis insisted.

Jonas sighed. He leaned his face forward, reaching up with his right hand. He slipped the mask up over his head and then raised his face to her. His hair was dark and wavy though now no longer carefully combed, disheveled as it was from removing his mask. His face still looked young to her as it was the type of face that would never look old, but there were lines at the corners of his gray-green eyes that she had not noticed on their previous encounters.

It was the paisley-shaped bruise around his right eye that made her catch her breath. It was darker and more pronounced than she remembered it, with a number of abrasions on his cheek that she did not remember him having before. Instinctively, she reached up with her hand toward his injured cheek.

He pulled away from her reach.

"Did Merrick do this to you?" Ellis asked.

"No." Jonas shook his head. "You said you remembered me. What do you remember?"

"I remember a watchmaker's shop," Ellis said. Even as she spoke the words, she could almost feel the cool of the

cabinet glass and smell the lacquer from the clock hous-
ings on the wall. "My watch was not running and I was
trying to keep an appointment with . . ."

"With some suitor your mother had arranged for
you." Jonas smiled at her.

"Yes." Ellis nodded. "I never kept the appointment."

"I pretended to take a long time fixing your watch,"
Jonas said with a shy smile. "I didn't want you to leave
and certainly not to meet another man."

"Hmm." Ellis conveyed neither approval nor disdain
with the sound, just acknowledgment of the statement.
She stepped around him, surveying their surroundings.
"This is the servants' hall, I believe. We're below stairs,
as my . . ."

Ellis stopped in thought.

"As your what?" Jonas urged.

Ellis smiled sadly as she stepped listlessly about the hall.
"As my mother used to say. I don't think she ever paid
much thought to the people who worked in places like
this. She certainly didn't approve of my being anywhere
near a kitchen."

"Which explains a great deal," Jonas said with a
gentle laugh.

"Whatever does that mean?" Ellis asked with a sharp
glance.

"Nothing at all," Jonas said. He leaned back against
the wall, setting his mask down on a bench next to him.

"Well, Mister . . . what is your name again?"

"Jonas," he replied with less patience than he felt. "Jonas Kirk."

"Well, Mr. Jonas Kirk of Boston—"

"Nova Scotia," Jonas corrected.

"I beg your pardon?" Ellis's eyes narrowed.

"I only worked in Boston, in my uncle's shop," Jonas corrected. "I was born in Nova Scotia."

"Well, then, Mr. Kirk," Ellis said, taking a step toward him. "I believe it's clear that we are no longer in either Boston or Nova Scotia now."

"No, we are very far from both, indeed." Jonas nodded. He shook himself out of the pleasant reverie. "Too far."

"And what do you propose?" Ellis asked, her eyes fixed on him. She still did not trust him any more than she trusted Merrick but the memory of their meeting lingered in her mind.

You have to learn the rules before you can break them.

Her father's voice.

"That we find Jenny, wherever she is in this house," Jonas said. "Please, Ellis. We haven't the time to stop now and talk."

"We find Jenny?" Ellis mocked. "Slipping unnoticed about this house in our masquerade clown costumes so that we might find my cousin before one of the other lunatics finds her first. And once we do?"

"Once we find Jenny, we'll know what to do," Jonas

said with increasing urgency. "Please. We need to move on, Ellis. If we stay in one place too long, they'll find us."

"Move on?" Ellis raised her eyebrow at the thought. "Find Jenny, you say, and move on to where?"

"Home," Jonas replied. "I need to get you home."

"Home? And I suppose you know where home is?"

"Yes, Ellis," Jonas said. "I've waited a very long time to take you there."

"And just what do you know of home?" Ellis asked, gesturing about her. "I have been told repeatedly that this is my home. This never-ending nightmare of senseless-ness. I am supposed to be some sort of queen of this asy-lum from what I understand. The lady of Echo House and the mistress of madness."

"You are indeed, my lady," said the chirping, nasal voice behind her.

Ellis turned around, startled.

Standing in the center of the servants' hall was an older woman wearing the plain, black dress common among the servants. Her hair was stark white and carefully pulled back into a bun at the back of her head. She had a square face softened by age. Her eyes were a deep blue, spar-kling behind a pince-nez perched across the bridge of her nose.

"I'm sorry for having startled you, ma'am," the old woman said gently. Her raised hand was as pale as linen and as thin as parchment. "I heard voices here in the hall

and thought I might be of some assistance to your ladyship. And the boy is right, my lady, about one thing: you
really must hurry along."

"Who are you?" Ellis demanded.

"Beggin' your pardon, ma'am," the woman said with
a slight curtsy. "I'm your housekeeper . . . Mrs. Crow."

7

MRS. CROW

"Mrs. Crow?"

The older woman folded her hands in front of her and cocked her head slightly to one side. "But of course your ladyship would not be remembering me, having just returned so far from outside the house. It is completely understandable and you shouldn't trouble yourself about it. You are as always welcome here, your ladyship, but I am surprised to see you below stairs. I'd offer her ladyship a cup of tea but if he's after you again then you've no time to lose."

"Who?" Ellis struggled to regain her composure. "Who is after us?"

"Why, I suspect Lord Merrick is at your heels again," Mrs. Crow said with a demure smile. "Was not his lordship the reason you fled the house in the first place?"

"I don't . . . I don't recall," Ellis said as she shook her head slightly, her eyes fixed on the woman. Mrs. Crow had every appearance of benign servitude. Her smile was pleasant. There was a slight rosy blush to her cheeks. Her dress was clean and neatly pressed with a style that was simple and unadorned. She might as easily have fit the role of someone's doting grandmother. As for the position of housekeeper, Ellis was hard-pressed to imagine anyone more perfectly suited for the role. Yet there was something about her, something that Ellis could not put into words, that raised the hair at the back of her neck as she spoke to the older woman.

"Well, I most certainly *do* recall," Mrs. Crow said cheerfully.

"Ellis, let's go," Jonas urged. His eyes were fixed on Mrs. Crow, his face a mask of disapproval.

"In those?" Mrs. Crow considered Ellis's Columbine costume, an abrupt laugh bursting from her lips, which she quickly stifled. "You can hardly pass unnoticed."

"Our departure was somewhat unplanned," Ellis commented with a glance toward Jonas.

"Well, we shall have to do something about that." Mrs. Crow raised her right hand slightly, her index finger barely extended. Her eyes shifted their gaze slightly to Ellis's left. "Margaret?"

"Yes, Mrs. Crow."

Ellis jumped slightly within her skin, startled by the sudden appearance of the young woman at her elbow. She had last seen Margaret as they were rushing past her in the theater several floors above them and a dizzying number of hallways between. Yet, at the mere mention of her name by Mrs. Crow, Margaret had appeared at her side in a seeming instant.

"Margaret, her ladyship will be needing something to wear for the evening," Mrs. Crow said, appraising Ellis with a set of critical eyes.

"May I suggest something casual," Margaret offered, her eyes fixed on Ellis's astonished and concerned countenance. "Something she can move about in at her ease."

"That would be quite satisfactory," Mrs. Crow agreed. "Perhaps a traveling suit?"

"I believe I know just such an outfit, ma'am," Margaret responded with a sideways glance at Ellis. "If her ladyship will kindly follow me back—"

"NO!" Ellis's single word echoed down the interminable servants' hall, leaving a shocked silence in its wake.

Mrs. Crow raised her white eyebrows as she turned to the lady's maid. "I believe, Margaret, that her ladyship prefers not to be seen in public at the moment. She might wish to avoid any awkward encounters in the private quarters. If you would be so kind as to fetch her ladyship a suitable outfit and bring it at once to my own room, that would be satisfactory."

"But Mrs. Crow," Margaret protested, "I am her lady's maid and it is my duty to—"

"Do as you're told, girl." The deep blue of Mrs. Crow's

eyes fixed on the lady's maid, a chill firmness edging her voice. "I'll brook no nonsense from you today. Be quick about it and not a word to anyone about Lady Ellis. Her ladyship may have a long journey ahead of her and cannot be delayed by a single moment."

"Yes, ma'am," Margaret replied with a surly tone.

"And Jonas," Ellis added, turning to call after Margaret as she hurried down the hall. "He'll need a change of clothing as well before we . . . Where is he?"

"Jonas, of course," Mrs. Crow replied cheerily. "He's our hallboy. New, really, and I don't know as to whether he is going to work out. He tends to come and go at his own liking."

"But he was just here," Ellis insisted.

"And I've sent him to change, as your ladyship commands," said Mrs. Crow as she bowed slightly and motioned for Ellis to follow her down the hall. "I'm sure he'll return at once. I'll have a word with him when he does. For now, would your ladyship join me until Margaret arrives? She won't be but a moment. I promise no one will come looking for you in my room and this old woman is in the mood to reminisce."

Reminisce? Ellis considered a concept for a moment: how did one reminisce without memories? Yet she *had* remembered something.

Hold still, Ellie, and the butterflies will come to you.

Another memory and clearer this time. She had been running for days, it seemed, trying to escape a house that seemed without end. Now holding still, learning the rules of this new game and recovering her thoughts was bringing her more success. This kindly appearing servant might help her connect with more. She was the first person she had encountered since she awoke on the train so long ago who was willing to talk to her about the past. Surely only good, she decided, could come from further remembrance.

As she followed Mrs. Crow down the hall, she thought she could hear the receding sound of frantically beating moth wings against the window glass of the kitchen behind her.

Ellis frowned at the dress laid out on the narrow bed. It was the same ugly traveling suit she had worn on the train when she first came to herself in this place. It was heavy, woolen and, in her opinion, deeply unfashionable. She had worn it, too, when she fled into the rain from Summersend searching for refuge in the Norumbega. She wore that miserable, wet and stained outfit in her desperate run through the endless rooms of this maddening house until Margaret had found her. Now, here Margaret had presented her again with this same dress. At least now it was clean and pressed although how Margaret had managed it during the time she had been in her ridiculous clown costume, Ellis could not imagine.

"Is there something the matter, your ladyship?" asked Mrs. Crow, standing in the doorway behind her.

"No, not at all," Ellis said, swallowing hard.

"You were always fond of the costume parties," Mrs. Crow said with a quivering sigh. She reached up from behind Ellis, pulling out the hairpins securing the hat to Ellis's hair and lifting it free. She set the hat carefully down on the top of a small chest of drawers to their right. "You often told me that you created this house just so that you might hold such grand events."

"So, this house . . . Echo House . . . you say I created it?" Ellis asked, reaching up to the ruff, trying to feel how it was attached to the collar of the jacket.

"Oh, dear me, yes," Mrs. Crow replied with a happy chuckle. She moved to the rocking chair set with barely enough space in the corner of the room and settled slowly into it as she spoke. "Of course, it wasn't your first Day. There were a great many others before and, my, some of them were so very fanciful indeed! I think you made more scrapbooks than anyone and never quite seemed to be satisfied with how any of them turned out. You won the Game more often than even Merrick. He always found you a real challenge."

Ellis was feeling a little dizzy trying to find the meaning in the housekeeper's words, let alone follow along. "So, this Game that everyone plays. It has rules?"

"Everything has rules, my lady," said Mrs. Crow.

"How did we get here?" Ellis asked. "In the Game, I mean."

"Oh, that's an old story, your ladyship," Mrs. Crow sighed, leaning until her back came to rest against the wall. "Way before the house ever was."

"Tell it to me," Ellis insisted.

"Well, best I can remember, there was this fight between two brothers," said Mrs. Crow as her eyes narrowed. "One was noble and wanted discipline and order for all of us, to give us purpose. The other was selfish and wanted to do whatever he liked. But their father said we all had to decide for ourselves which of them we were going to follow: the noble one or the selfish one. Some chose one and some chose the other but there were a few who didn't want to decide at all. Those are the people who came here to the Tween. Those are the folks who are in the Game."

"So everyone here is part of the Game?" Ellis asked.

"I didn't say that, ma'am," Mrs. Crow corrected gently.

"But you said . . ."

"I said that those were the folks that came to the Tween and are in the Game," Mrs. Crow replied, straightening up to perch on the edge of the chest. "There are others who have come to the Tween for their own purposes. There are emissaries—some call them angels and some call them demons—who make their way into the Tween trying get some soul to finally make that choice they didn't want to make in the first place and ally themselves with one brother or the other."

"So, what is the Game?" Ellis asked.

"Well, it's a place that we all share." Mrs. Crow smiled. "It's a way for us to enjoy a taste of life for a bit."

"You mean a better life, don't you, Mrs. Crow?"

"Isn't that what I said? Here, now, let me assist your ladyship," said the housekeeper with a kindly, sweet smile. Mrs. Crow stood up and stepped around behind Ellis. She reached forward toward the buttons that closed the back of the costume, her pale, white fingers remarkably deft at the task. The back of the costume parted, exposing Ellis's back to the chill of the room.

Ellis shivered.

"Oh, and you have such shoulders," Mrs. Crow said admiringly. "Have you thought where you might go?"

"I need to find Jenny before I do anything," Ellis said simply, then turned around to face Mrs. Crow. "Do you know Jenny?"

"Miss Jenny? Of course, my lady." Mrs. Crow chuckled with merriment. "Your sister, as I recall."

"Odd," Ellis remarked. "She was my cousin last time . . ."

"Cousin . . . sister . . . it makes little difference in the end, does it not, my lady?" Mrs. Crow managed to get the last of the buttons undone. "Have you thought where you might start?"

"I hardly know where I am, let alone where I might begin," Ellis sighed.

"Well, if I might be so bold with her ladyship, might

I make a suggestion?" Mrs. Crow prattled on, her eyes twinkling. She did not wait for a response to her question. "I would begin in the Old Quarter. There are many places there where someone might hide and few here in this house that go there. It reminds them of the past and I think it makes them uncomfortable. Still, you've got a guide in that Jonas and that could make all the difference."

Ellis stepped out of the costume and turned with no small reluctance to the drab green outfit that was so irritatingly familiar to her that lay across the narrow bed.

"And one more word, if I may," Mrs. Crow said, stepping back and once more crossing her hands in front of her. "That young man Jonas . . ."

Mrs. Crow paused.

"What is it, Mrs. Crow?"

"I hesitate to say, my lady," the old woman said through a troubled frown. "It's not my place . . ."

"Go on," Ellis insisted.

"Well, it's true that he knows something about the Ruins . . . the Old Quarter of the house, I mean," the elderly woman said, her words coming slow and with caution. "But he may be a bit too familiar with them, if you know what I mean."

"I'm sure I don't." Ellis glared at Mrs. Crow. "Go on."

"I'm just saying that some places in the Ruins are not safe," Mrs. Crow said, holding her pale hands up. "You'll need him to help you find Miss Jenny but he's not playing the same Game as the rest of us . . . or you, for that matter,

my lady. In the end, it'll be only Jonas that Jonas is thinking about saving. Mark my words."

Ellis picked up the drab, green jacket of the traveling
suit from off of the bed, gazing at it thoughtfully. "In the
end, Mrs. Crow, aren't we all just trying to save ourselves?"

The double doors were still open onto the large garden
courtyard. The stones of the path were wet from the rain
that had finally ceased. The leaves of the trimmed bushes
glistened slightly under the light from the windows of the
floors above. The muffled sound of distant laughter drifted
down from those same windows, carefree and oblivious
around the figure of Mrs. Crow.

She stood in the open doorway watching two figures
moving quietly into the hedge maze that filled the courtyard. One was a man dressed in the house livery of a
servant, an outfit completely unsuited for the task before
them, but Mrs. Crow had insisted that the young man
maintain his station. The other was a woman in a traveling dress who stopped at the edge of the entrance to the
maze and turned for one last look.

Mrs. Crow smiled and waved encouragingly at her.

She raised her hand in acknowledgment and in a
moment both the man and woman were gone.

Beyond the maze rose the dark and forbidding wing
of the house known as the Old Quarter or, more com-
monly, the Ruins. They were not ruins, in the strictest

sense of the word, Mrs. Crow corrected herself, but simply abandoned to the decay of memory. The windows there were dark and as hollow as the grave.

Mrs. Crow lingered at the threshold.

Waiting.

"Are they gone?" came the deep voice from the dark hall behind her.

"Yes, my lord." Mrs. Crow spoke without turning at all, her gaze still cast over the garden. "As I told you they would be. Everything is in place and I have sown the seeds of doubt between them. It will just take a little time for them to take root. That was always part of the plan."

"But not sending them into the Ruins!" Merrick stepped from the shadows, his face grim as he came to stand beside her.

Mrs. Crow turned toward him, her blue eyes taking on a dull, featureless black color. Her words were as sharp as cold steel.

"Are you questioning my scheme?" Mrs. Crow spoke the quiet words with such authority that they caused the small windows framed in the door to quake. Around them both, shadows began to gather into terrible forms with leathery wings and long sharp claws, their blank eyes turning to stare at Merrick.

"No, not at all, Mrs. Crow," Merrick said with careful words as he took a step back. "I am just observing that you never said you would send them into the old part of the house."

"True enough, Lord Merrick," the old woman said with a suddenly gentle, demure smile. The horrendous shadows around them faded from existence. "But that is where she will discover the most terrible thing of all, the one thing that she cannot fight and from which she can never flee."

"Indeed?" Merrick raised an inquisitive eyebrow. "And what is this terrible monster she will find?"

"The truth about herself," Mrs. Crow said gently.

"The truth?" Merrick frowned.

"Yes," Mrs. Crow chuckled through her malicious grin. "And it will destroy them both."

Mrs. Crow turned and stepped back into the servants' hall.

Merrick followed after her.

Neither of them noticed a third figure slip into the garden maze behind them.

8

THE GARDEN

Ellis looked up at the leaden sky. It had gotten lighter as the morning progressed but there were no breaks in the clouds. It had been dark when they first entered the garden but that now seemed ages in the past. What had at first appeared to be a simple garden maze had proven to be more devious and convoluted than she had imagined. The neat, trimmed hedges they had first encountered had slowly and increasingly given way to hoarier shrubs. The carefully trimmed grass beneath their feet now reached up around Ellis's knees. What had looked like a simple and brisk walk across a small garden was turning into a wilderness expedition.

"This is ridiculous," Jonas said through clenched teeth as he pushed past the rough corner of an overgrown hedge. "What was Mrs. Crow thinking? Asking me to dress in this footman's livery. Did she think we were going on a picnic brunch?"

"I'm sure that I don't know what Mrs. Crow was thinking," Ellis said in return, her reply perhaps a little more brusque than she intended. Ellis reached across her jacket, lifting her small pocket watch into view. She frowned at its face. "It's ten before nine in the morning. Just how far can it be to the other side of a courtyard garden?"

"That depends," Jonas said, "on how far it needs to be."

She could see the gables and ridgelines of the roof of the house on the far side of the garden court but little else. The hedges of the garden maze obstructed any more complete vision of the Ruins. Even the clouds overhead had lowered to obscure the topmost spires. What was worse, despite being able to see their destination, the increasingly unkempt hedges were twisting their course. Although they could see the slate tiles of the roof, it seemed to her that they were no closer to reaching them with every step than they were before.

"Are you certain this is the way?" Ellis asked.

"Yes, this is the way," Jonas replied at once, as though daring anyone to defy the statement.

"How can you be certain?" Ellis pressed him to answer as they were confronted suddenly with another intersection of passages to the left and the right. The two paths before them both led into trellis tunnels on either side that twisted into even darker regions beyond. The vines covering them were overgrown, making both directions dark and forbidding.

"Because this is a different kind of garden maze," Jonas said, considering which direction to take. "We don't solve this maze . . . the maze solves us."

"What are you talking about?" Ellis shook her head, wondering if she had heard him correctly.

"What I mean is that it's not about going right or left so much as going right or wrong," Jonas continued as he deliberated. "It's about who we are, not where we go."

"That makes no sense."

"And you're expecting sense in a place like this?" Jonas raised his eyebrow in the dark, paisley-shaped mark over his eye. They looked again down the two divergent paths. "I think this may be it."

"May be what?"

"The entrance to the maze."

"But we've been in the maze for hours now." Ellis shook her head.

"Try to stay close to me." Jonas turned to face her, his eyes searching her own. "If we get separated, I promise I'll meet you on the other side."

"*If* we get separated?" Exasperation crept in to color her words. "You're supposed to be my guide through all of this!"

"Please believe me, Ellis, I am here to help you but there are some things—some places—that you have to manage alone. It will be all right," he promised, though he failed to hide the pain in his eyes. His strong hands took her by both shoulders. "You can do this. Please remember that I told you that you could do this, wherever the maze takes you. Promise me!"

"Let go of me," Ellis demanded. "You're hurting me."

"Promise me," Jonas insisted.

"I promise," she snarled.

"What," Jonas insisted. "What did you promise me?"

"You know very well what I promised!" Ellis said with indignation and more loudly than needful. She relaxed and corrected herself. "I mean, I'll remember that *you said* I could do this."

Jonas laughed slightly, his hands releasing her from his firm grip. "That temper. I never would have guessed that I would actually miss it. You were always so careful with words, Ellis, except when you were mad."

"Angry," Ellis said without thinking. "You meant 'except when I was angry.'"

"Still correcting me, too, eh?" Jonas said, his smile diminishing slightly. "So, Ellis, which way do we go?"

"Which way?"

"Yes . . . Left or right?"

"*You're* supposed to be the guide," Ellis said. "Isn't choosing *your* job?"

"It won't make any difference, Ellis," Jonas quietly urged her. "Just choose."

Ellis was finding the situation more exasperating by the moment. She turned, peering down each of the paths.

Both wound out of sight into near complete darkness. Each seemed equally forbidding.

"You say they both lead to the Ruins?" Ellis asked.

"Yes, they both lead to the old part of the house," Jonas confirmed.

"Then let's go left," Ellis said.

"Left it is." Jonas nodded, reaching out and taking Ellis by the hand.

Ellis snatched her hand back, still smarting from Jonas's teasing as they came to the first turn in the vine trellis. She turned the corner. Here the dark tunnel, sparsely dappled with sunlight, branched in three directions.

Jonas had vanished.

"Jonas?" she spoke into the silence of the garden.

No one answered her in return.

"Jonas," she called again.

"Ellie!"

Ellis turned toward the sound. It came from the left most of the vine-covered maze halls. It sounded distant to her ears, muffled and indistinct yet she was sure it was her name.

"Jonas?" she repeated, her voice sounding more uncertain than before. She took several hesitant steps into the left branch of the vine-covered trellis tunnel. She could see that its dark passage was lit only by a half-dozen thin shafts of light that had managed to penetrate the thick leaves of the covering vines. It ran straight for something like fifty feet, the thin shafts of brilliant light making it difficult to gauge the distance. There it turned sharply to the right.

Ellis took another step. "Jonas? Where are you?"

She froze, staring.

A dark figure was staring back at her from the dim far distance of the corridor. She thought it was a little girl or boy, she could not tell at this distance, and poor. The features of its face were indiscernible. Ellis was reminded strongly of the little child on the lighthouse island that she had seen through the telescope at Summersend whose face she also had never seen. She had wondered about that child as well but now this figure was haunting and disturbing, staring back at her, unmoving and unmoved.

Ellis swallowed and gathered up her courage to speak to the still figure staring back at her from the shadows veiling its eyes. "Hello? Are you lost?"

The child shifted its weight slowly from one foot to the other.

"Ellie! I'm here! Come find me!"

The voice startled Ellis. It was not coming from the child but from somewhere farther along beyond it. It was familiar to her, still muffled and distant. A man's voice— deep and warm.

The shadowed child at the end of the hall turned and ran, vanishing almost at once from Ellis's eyes.

"Wait! Child!" Ellis called out. She plunged into the vine corridor after the faceless child. "Come back! I want to talk to you!"

Ellis ran down the length of the dark vine tunnel in-
tent on seeing the face of the child. She came to a quick
succession of junctions in the maze, at each catching just
a glimpse of the child as it dodged down another branching path. She could hear the child laughing up ahead, a
bright, delighted sound all jumbled with the deep reso-
nance of the voice always ahead of her.

*"Come along, Ellie! You've almost got me! You can do it,
Ellie!"*

Ellis felt a wrenching in her soul that was too wonderful and dreadful for her to bear. Yet she rushed on-
ward after the child always before her in the maze and
just out of reach.

"Wait!" she called out. "Stop!"

She turned a corner again and suddenly emerged into a
large garden space in the middle of the maze. She stopped,
her eyes squinting slightly in the suddenly brighter
space.

Her eyes quickly grew accustomed. Here, the nearly
overgrown garden had been immaculately groomed and
dressed. The hedge walls of the rectangular area were
trimmed into beautiful symmetry; the grass beneath her
feet was painstakingly short and uniformly trim. The
edges of the flower beds were crisp lines and filled with
flowers, whose colors were only muted by the dull sky
overhead.

"I . . . I know this garden," Ellis murmured to herself.
"I've been here before."

"There you are, my little Ellie!"

Ellis turned sharply toward the voice at the other end of the garden. She caught her breath, tears welling up in her eyes.

He was tall and thin; all arms and legs as he used to jokingly tease her. It was a too-oft-repeated joke between them that had long become more endearing than amusing. He stood in his evening dress, his starched wing collar shirt undone and his white bow tie draped around the back of his neck. The buttons on his white waistcoat were undone although he still wore his black dress coat. There were grass stains on his shoes, which her mother would scold him about before they left for the evening. He had left his top hat in the front hall so that he would not forget it. Ellis remembered she had been so upset about her parents leaving for another in an unending stream of social functions that she had tried to make them stay home by hiding in the garden until they were too late for their party to leave.

Now he stood at the other end of the hedged garden just as she remembered him from when she was seven years old. His hair was mostly black and only barely showing signs of a receding hairline. His mustache was dark and full. His eyes were bright with merriment for he loved her so and, though she did not know it at the time, relished any excuse to play with her.

"Papa." Ellis breathed the word out as a sigh.

Charles Murry Harkington's smile was genuine, warm

and broad with joy when he saw his daughter at the other end of the garden plot.

"Ellie!" her papa said with delight. "There you are! Playing a game in the garden, are we?"

"Papa!" Ellis's lower lip trembled as she uttered the word again. She did not dare move for fear that the vision would be broken, that her father would vanish and take her heart with him as he had once before.

"Ellie, my girl," he said. "Can you catch me? It's my turn, Ellie! See if you can catch me!"

They had played a game. He had coaxed her back to the house that evening with a game.

"No, Papa!" Ellis cried out. "Please don't . . ."

"Come on, my girl!" her papa called out as he turned, the tails on his coat flying outward from his waist as he spun on his heels. "You'll not catch me!"

Her father ran away from her, running through the gap in the hedge at the far end of the garden.

"NO!" Ellis screamed. She ran quickly across the open lawn, plunging back into the hedge maze beyond.

She caught a glimpse of her father to her right, his coattails flapping behind him as he loped along, glancing backward toward her to make sure she was following him. She wheeled to the right in pursuit, running headlong and heedless.

"Papa!" she screamed, tears flowing freely from her eyes, blurring her vision. "Stop! Wait for me!"

She wheeled around another corner of the maze, the

trimmed branches of the hedge stinging her arm as she brushed against them. He was there again, closer this time but still more than ten steps ahead of her. She lost track of the turns they made through the maze. She ran with abandon, her heart beating against her chest, her lungs aching. Still her father remained ahead of her at every step. She could see with every glance backward at her that the lines in his face were growing deeper and more care-worn. His hair was receding and growing grayer at the temples with every step. His paunch, too, was growing yet somehow he always remained just out of reach of her.

"Catch me, my girl!" he called out, his voice growing more raspy and thin. "Almost there, my little Ellie! You almost have me!"

The clouds overhead had grown darker and more menacing. Ellis took no notice. The sound of thunder came closer by the moment and the world darkened as they sped through the maze.

"Almost, Ellie!" her father called laughingly to her. "You'll catch me yet, girl!"

She was within a few steps of him.

The rain began to fall.

He turned a corner before her and she followed at his heels.

They ran out of the hedge. The rain obscured the distance but Ellis could see enough to know they had entered a small park in the garden. There was the veiled shape of trees by the side of a river to her left and a tall folly built in the shape of the Pantheon in Rome ahead of them.

She heard her father laugh.

Ellis lunged forward, grasping her father's arm and pulling him into her embrace.

Bronze.

Ellis shivered, her arms still wrapped around the chill figure.

Her father was made of bronze.

She let go, tumbling awkwardly backward through the air and landing painfully on her side against the wet ground. She looked up at the figure, now fixed atop a carved granite block, the shape of which she knew only too well.

His epitaph. His headstone.

His monument.

9

ALICIA'S FOLLY

Ellis rolled painfully to sit up on the sodden ground. Her tears mixed with the rain falling about her, lost in the pools atop the already soaked ground. She sobbed, water flowing around her open mouth, her shoulders slumped forward in her newly discovered grief. She remembered her father—her papa—and now she sat at the foot of the cold and unforgiving monument to the man who had showed her a father's love and left her alone before she was ready for the world.

Ellis felt as though her heart would break. A flood of impressions, disjointed and incomplete, burst into her mind in quick succession. Her father's smile at her wearing her party dress. The hurt in his eyes when she had lied to him about the broken vase in his study. The bent shoulder and tears—her father's tears—when the Jensen boy died under his care and all he could do was hold her so tightly that she thought she might break. Sitting in his lap in his study, the sound of his deep voice reading to her from *Tom Sawyer* because her mother was out for the evening . . .

"*Ellie!*" Her father's voice was dull and distant through the rain. "*El-lie!*"

She drew in a shuddering breath.

He was gone. She loved him and she believed that he had loved her as best he knew how. She had wished he could have told her in so many words but that was not his way. She had chased his approval all her life and he was gone before she heard it from his lips.

"*Ellis!*"

It was a whisper through the rushing sound around her. The rain was falling now in torrents, obscuring even the frozen figure of her father into a darker shape against the gray of the deluge falling about her. It seemed like her father's voice but it was not coming from the statue. Ellis began noticing other shapes, like shadows of wind-swept trees shifting in the rain about her, far enough so that she could make nothing more of them than their vague forms.

"*Ellis! Come . . . It is your turn . . .*"

She scrambled to her feet, her high-button shoes slipping slightly against the soaked ground. She turned, trying to discern the direction from which the voice was speaking to her.

"Ellis! Come on. They're waiting for you . . ."

Ellis looked up once more at the cold, bronze figure of her father towering in the rain above her. She had hated to visit his grave though her mother had insisted each Sunday. Each time she could not help but know that her father was not found in the chill metal or even beneath the frozen ground. He was anywhere but here.

She caught up her hat from off the ground and set its sodden form firmly on her head. She wiped the water from her eyes, squinting into the torrent, believing that somehow it would help her pierce the veil of gray falling about her. Just at the edge of her vision, she caught movement in the rain, shifting shadows just at the edge of her vision that disappeared when she turned her gaze directly on them.

"Who are you?" she cried out, her voice muted in the rain. "What do you want?"

"Ellis, everyone has to take their turn . . ."

She swallowed. She could not be certain where the voices were coming from through the rain. Indeed, now that she considered, she was not all that certain that the shapes she was seeing were actually there. They might be some trick of the light in the downpour, shadows of phantoms that existed only in her own mind.

Whatever they were, she realized she needed shelter from the increasing savagery of the storm. She cast her eyes about again and soon set her gaze on a great shadow fixed in the veil of the storm.

The folly.

Ellis could just make out the dim form across the park grass. She staggered toward it, struggling to keep her feet under her in the downpour. As she approached, the shape grew more distinct and solid. She could make out the broad steps of its porch and the towering columns that formed a colonnade around the perimeter of the structure. She quickly climbed the slick granite stairs and slowed her steps as she approached the rectangular doorway that led into the interior of the folly.

The exterior of the folly had been patterned after the Pantheon in Rome and the interior followed the theme. There was an oculus cut into the pinnacle of the dome, a round opening that permitted a dim shaft of light to penetrate the interior.

Ellis followed the shaft of dull light down from the oculus opening to where it rested on a stone bier that was made of polished stone as black as night. The jittering flash of lightning suddenly illuminated the bier in stark light. A figure lay atop it, draped in white. It was face up with its arms resting along either side as though in stately repose. She could not see the face, for it was covered by the sheet. The rain poured down through the oculus opening overhead directly down onto the figure and its bier, running down it to be collected in a pool around the base of the bier. Here, the waters poured into a surrounding trough that carried the water away down through underground pipes.

Ellis listened to the rain. It continued to pound against the stones overhead and the ground behind her.

She drew in a long breath and blew it out.

Ellis took a step toward the bier.

"Miss Harkington! We're waiting!"

Ellis turned with a start toward the voice barking in her right ear. The sounds of the rain were suddenly silenced.

She was no longer in the folly.

She was in the amphitheater of Boston Medical College.

She stood at the open end of the U shape that formed the enormous operating room in the school. Arranged above the floor were eight concourses, each following the same shape and accessed by steep stairs. The warm color of their polished wood was accentuated by the six gas lamps suspended from a framework that hung over the center of the room from a long pipe mounted to the ceiling. Large skylights also might have admitted light into the space but for the storm howling and moaning against them. The rain had inexplicably turned into a winter snow squall.

Ellis remembered it had snowed that day, too. It had been a bitter winter and even Boston Harbor was in danger of freezing solid.

The benches surrounding the operating theater were more occupied than she might have expected. Certainly there were students here who were not part of her class. Someone had spread word of what was happening today and it had drawn a greater attendance from the medical students than might normally attend. Dr. Donnelly, her instructor in gross anatomy, was glaring at her impatiently from where he stood on the far side of the operating table in the center of the room. He wore a surgical apron over his shirt and tie, his sleeves rolled up past his elbows as he stood with his arms crossed over his chest. Dr. Donnelly had a bushy, gray mustache beneath a wide nose, his dark eyes gazing at her in his ever-critical manner. His spats over his polished shoes were bright white and Ellis knew woe betide anyone who caused a stain to fall on them.

Ellis glanced down at herself. She was still in the drab, green traveling suit, now dripping rainwater on the floor of the operating theater. She took off her soaked hat with a slight feeling of embarrassment for having entered the room in front of all the other students with it still on her head.

"Well, Miss Harkington?" scowled Dr. Donnelly. "Your patient may have all day but the rest of us certainly do not!"

Laughter rippled among the students gazing down from the benches onto the floor of the operating room.

"Yes, Doctor," Ellis said as she turned her attention to the operating table locked atop the pedestal in the center of the room. A white sheet lay over it, its contours easily recognized as being draped over a body. The feet were exposed from beneath the bottom of the sheet but covering the face at the top.

My patient, Ellis thought with a scowl on her face. *My patient can be patient indeed . . . seeing as they are already dead.*

Ellis looked about her for a surgical apron but found none. An instrument stand stood next to the operating table. She recognized a number of bone saws, retractors and scalpels. They appeared to be well sharpened and clean. A second table, longer, stood to one side. There, a number of metal bowls were arranged, each one gleaming brightly under the gas lamps overhead.

"When you are quite ready!" Dr. Donnelly snapped.

Ellis looked up sharply. "I'm quite ready, Doctor."

Donnelly gave a curt nod, then turned to address the students in the gallery. "Knowing why someone has died is an imperative aspect of your chosen profession. How can one hope to keep someone alive if they do not understand what kills? We discover the cause of death through the process of an autopsy. It is one of the few procedures that a doctor can perform without risk to the patient."

Dr. Donnelly laughed at his own stale joke. The students in the gallery knew enough to chuckle diplomatically.

The operating theater felt familiar to Ellis but there was also something of a sense of dread about it. She knew this was somehow a memory of her past that was playing out again for her in this bizarre place. Something she had regretted. Something of which she was ashamed. But it lay at the edge of her memory, just beyond the next moment in time.

Ellis reached for the top edge of the sheet covering the corpse with both hands.

"The first part of the process involves cataloging the particulars of the subject." Dr. Donnelly had turned his voice toward the more familiar mode of lecturing that so often put his students to sleep. "In this case, we know that the individual is a white male, sixty-four inches in height weighing two hundred and thirty-six pounds . . ."

Ellis pulled the sheet downward away from the face and chest toward the corpse's waist.

The students roared with laughter.

Ellis caught her breath, blushed without volition and hastily tossed the edge of the sheet back. It did not cover the face but fell only as far as the body's shoulders.

"Very funny." Dr. Donnelly scowled once more.

Ellis's hands shook as she stood, her gaze fixed on the face staring straight upward from the table.

"I see that my students have too much time on their hands." Dr. Donnelly stepped to the foot of the operating table and lifted the paper tag tied to the corpse's toe. "Then let us consider instead this white female, sixty-seven inches in height, one hundred and twelve pounds, approximately twenty-two years of age. The body is cold and unembalmed. No readily apparent lividity or rigor. Signs of some blunt-force trauma in the posterior cranial region but otherwise no other unexpected or unusual external markings . . ."

The corneas of the eyes were cloudy. The hair was wet and matted where it was splayed on the table beneath her head, but Ellis knew at once the identity of the body lying on the operating table before her.

"Having completed the external examination, we now move on to the—"

"I need another body," Ellis blurted out.

"What?" Dr. Donnelly was not used to being interrupted, especially by a student.

"Please, Dr. Donnelly," Ellis pleaded. "If we could just . . . just get a different body from the morgue . . ."

Sniggering laughter passed as an undercurrent through the observation gallery. Ellis blushed. One or more of her fellow students had substituted this body for the one she had expected. She was doing exactly what they had intended her to do: embarrass herself before their instructor.

"There's no time for that!" Dr. Donnelly insisted. "Just carry on with this one!"

"Her name is Alicia," Ellis said, trying to remain calm. "I know her."

"Nonsense! The body is listed as a Jane Doe," Donnelly said pointedly. "And even if you did know her, it shouldn't make any difference! If you're going to ever become a practicing physician, do you really expect to only have strangers die for you?"

The laughter in the gallery was hearty now.

"No, Doctor," Ellis replied. "Of course not."

"Then let's get on with this, shall we?" Dr. Donnelly said with barely an effort toward patience. "As I was saying, having completed the external examination, we now move on to an examination of the internal organs of the chest and bowels. This is important as there is no obvious external cause of death. The first step of this process is to make a Y-shaped incision through the skin beginning from each of the shoulders down to the breastbone and continuing down the center of the body to the pubic bone. As we're dealing with a female subject, I suggest making the slant cut from the shoulders around the top of each breast before opening up the center. We'll then pull the skin flap at the top of the chest to toward the face and the two side flaps of skin to either side, exposing the rib cage and abdominal cavity. Note to use the scalpel to make quick cuts to separate the skin from the underlying tissue. It is also important to note any unusual odors that emanate from the body when the skin is pulled away as this may be an important clue should chemicals or drugs have been a factor in the death. Once the skin is pulled back, we'll use a bone saw to cut the ribs on either side and remove the rib cage to expose the chest cavity. Miss Harkington, please proceed to that point."

Ellis could hear muttered words and sniggering from the gallery above her. She drew in a breath and pulled the covering sheet back down around Alicia's waist. She hated to expose so publicly the skin of the woman she had known under the stark gaslight overhead and the prying eyes of the students leaning forward in the gallery.

There was something about the wet hair that bothered her. Had she drowned? If so, it was such a cold day, wouldn't that affect her body temperature?

Ellis turned dutifully toward the instrument table and selected the proper scalpel. She gripped it so tightly that her hand started to shake. She took in a deep breath and willed herself to relax slightly. Her hand stopped shaking.

I couldn't let them see how nervous I was, Ellis recalled. *I could not give those men in the room their smug satisfaction. I had to do it and hide what I felt.*

Ellis turned toward the operating table a little too quickly. Her hip bumped against the table, jostling it on its supporting pedestal. It was only the slightest of nudges but it was enough.

Alicia's head rolled to one side as though she were turning to look at Ellis. Her face stared back at her with haunting, dead eyes.

"The first cut down the center from the breast to the pubic bone needs to be firm and deep." Dr. Donnelly's words rang clearly in Ellis's mind even though her eyes were still fixed on returning the dead woman's stare. "You'll want to divert around the navel as it is particularly difficult to cut through."

Ellis held the scalpel raised in her frozen right hand. She could not look away from the dead face of Alicia staring back at her. *This is wrong. It wasn't Alicia on the table that*

day. That face was burned so deeply in my memory that I remem-
bered it in my worst dreams. She looked nothing like Alicia . . .

"Miss Harkington?" It was the voice of Dr. Donnelly.
"We're all waiting."

Ellis looked closer at the pallid face and the clouded
eyes of the woman.

A tear fell from the woman's eye.

She's not dead. The thought shouted in Ellis's mind as
though she were deaf to her own thoughts. *Everyone thinks
she is but she's not.*

"Miss Harkington!" Dr. Donnelly's voice was muffled
and distant, as though Ellis were underwater and her
professor were shouting at her from the surface. "I was
not in favor of your entering this school! A woman has
no place in this profession! You will complete this autopsy
or I will process your expulsion from this school myself."

Ellis's hand moved as it had in that operating theater
so long before. She was powerless to stop it then and she
was powerless to stop it now. As though moving through
water the blade descended toward the soft skin covering
the woman's sternum.

Ellis knew what was coming but was powerless to stop
it. The welling up of the blood as she made the long cut.
The woman's scream as she came suddenly to consciousness. Her thrashing on the table. The blood splatter on
Dr. Donnelly's spats. It was all moments away.

Where was her father when she needed him?

Gone . . . gone to his grave . . .

Her hand descended. The tip of the scalpel would not be denied biting into the flesh that beckoned it.

A hand reached out, grasping Ellis's right hand by the wrist.

Lightning flashed through the windows overhead.

The gallery, its students, Dr. Donnelly and the operating theater vanished. Ellis was surrounded by a cloud of dark, howling figures that retreated from her in all directions. Their cries faded almost at once and she could see where she was once more.

She stood in the rotunda of the folly next to the onyx bier. She was looking down at the terrified face of Alicia, her rain-wet face glistening in the occasional flashes of lightning through the oculus above.

Alicia was whimpering. "Please, Ellis . . . oh, please . . ."

Ellis shifted her gaze to her right hand suspended over Alicia's breast.

It held a gleaming scalpel.

A strong hand gripped Ellis's hand by the wrist, arresting its descent. The hold was strong and a little too tight.

It was Jonas's hand.

"It's all right, Ellis," Jonas said quietly. "You just need to relax now . . . and put that blade down."

Ellis's arm ached. She drew in a shuddering breath as she made an effort to relax.

"I told you, you could do this," Jonas said, pulling her hand down slowly. He took the scalpel from her hand.

"Yes," Ellis murmured, still shaken. "You told me."

Jonas turned to where Alicia lay shaking on the bier, the scalpel still in his hand. "You've been bound, Alicia. Just hold still and I'll cut you free. Who did this to you? Who left you here?"

"I . . . I don't know," Alicia said through quivering lips. "There was a fluttering sound like someone shaking a heavy curtain. There were shadows . . . lots of shadows . . . all coming toward me at once. I must have passed out . . . then I was here . . . and Ellis had that knife and . . . and . . ."

"That's enough, Alicia," Jonas said, his words soothing and reassuring. "Hold still. I'm about finished."

"Jonas," Ellis said. "Are we through the garden?"

"Yes," Jonas answered. "You're through."

"Will the Ruins be easier?" Ellis whispered.

Jonas did not answer.

10

RUINS OF THE PAST

Ellis stood at the threshold on the far side of the folly. She gazed between the columns across an unkempt patch of lawn surrounded by a hedge that had evidently not been tended to in a very long time. At the far edge of the lawn, she could see the dark, forbidding mass of the old section of the house veiled by the continuing rain.

The architecture struck her as a hodgepodge of styles, with little attempt at concern regarding the aesthetics of which might complement the other. On the main, it followed a combination of Georgian and Victorian shapes created out of brownstone but here and there were definite oddities. There was a classical Greek façade with Doric influence, its pediment broken with columns fallen on one side. Behind it rose a broken Gothic tower that leaned precariously to the left. The strange exterior extended seemingly forever in both directions, its ends fading into the torrential rain.

She could hear Jonas and Alicia stepping up behind her.

"Is that what they call 'the Ruins'?" Ellis asked.

"Yes," Jonas answered. "It's the old part of the house. The part you made once that has long since been abandoned."

"Merrick hates the place," Alicia added. "It reminds him too much of you."

Ellis turned toward Alicia.

You have to learn the rules before you can break them . . .

"And how is it that you were bound like a tragic gift so conveniently in my path?" Ellis asked, her eyes fixed on Alicia. "The last time I saw you was at Merrick's side. As I recall, you found my performance onstage rather amusing at the time."

"What choice did I have, Ellis?" Alicia looked down at the rain-slick stones of the folly's floor. "What choice do any of us have?"

"And so you just happened to be tied up on the bier?" Ellis's tone was both one of disbelief and accusation.

"Of course not!" Alicia's voice quivered as she spoke. "Merrick sent me into the maze after you. He said for me to follow you and find out what direction you were going in the Ruins. But I got lost . . . I don't know what happened. I got tangled up somehow trying to push through a trellis choked with vines. They grabbed me, wound around me . . . it was . . . it was . . ."

"It was the garden," Jonas said. "It was just trying to protect you, Ellis."

"Protect me?" Ellis scoffed.

"It *was* your garden." Jonas shrugged.

"Well, I don't much care for how it protects me!" Ellis snapped. A chill ran through her as she turned back to look across the lawn. She saw a set of stairs up to a small patio. The interior beyond the door was dark, their glass apparently broken. She could see the faint flutter of shredded curtains beyond the rusting panes. "Go back, Alicia. Be a good lapdog and tell your master that you found me and where we are—for all the good it will do him."

"No, Ellis," Alicia begged. "Please, don't make me go back. You left here once before . . . you can show us the way out again. I helped you . . . remember? Remember what I did for you?"

Ellis looked again at Alicia Van der Meer. She looked ridiculous in her Egyptian costume. The rain had smeared her makeup. She had lost her ornate headpiece and now her golden hair lay wet and heavy about her shoulders. Ellis remembered her in her stained, torn party dress running away from her on that street in Gamin a seeming eternity ago, giving Ellis time to flee while the hellish beast stalking them fell on Alicia with terrible fury.

Ellis turned to Jonas. "You know the way out of here?"

"I know someone who knows the way out." Jonas

nodded. "But we *have* to find Jenny first. Without her, it's pointless."

"And Jenny is in the Ruins?" Ellis urged.

"Yes, I have no doubt," Jonas affirmed.

"Why don't you doubt?" Ellis asked, her eyes fixed on Jonas. "Merrick hates the Ruins. Why would he hide her here?"

"I'm not convinced it was Merrick who hid her," Jonas answered. "I think he wants to find her as much as we do."

"Then the sooner we find her, the sooner this nightmare will end," Ellis said. She glanced at her ugly traveling suit and determined it could not become wetter than it was now. The sky was turning somewhat lighter under a rainy dawn. She stepped quickly into the rain, rushing toward the jagged, dark panes of the broken patio doors beyond the lawn.

Jonas glanced at Alicia and then followed quickly in Ellis's footsteps.

Alicia stood shivering at the edge of the folly.

"If you're coming, Alicia," Ellis called over her shoulder, "then come."

Alicia ran to follow after them.

Only the sound of glass crunching beneath the hard soles of her shoes greeted Ellis as she stepped cautiously through the open, rusting frame of one of the patio doors. Shards from the doors and the arched frames above it were everywhere on the floor, glinting in the gray light of the morning outside.

The rain had lightened up considerably and the dull light penetrating the clouds illuminated the long room. There were only the vestiges of curtains remaining in long, tattered rags on either side of the patio doors. The doors exiting the far side of the room were missing, the remaining hinges either twisted or missing altogether.

"What happened here?" Alicia asked from the patio doors, her eyes wide.

"Take care, Alicia," Jonas called quietly back to the young woman. "There is glass everywhere and I suspect those slippers you're wearing aren't terribly practical in this case."

"Well, could you please help me?" Alicia asked. "Just across the floor, I mean."

Jonas gave Ellis a questioning glance.

"Well, your costume isn't much better," Ellis observed. "Exploring ruins in servant's livery. At least your shoes are more sensible. You might as well carry her across."

Jonas nodded, stepping back to rescue the still-shivering woman standing in the rain just short of entering the room.

"It's odd that all the glass is broken. All of it is inside the room," Ellis muttered more to herself than to anyone else as she crossed to one of the oak doors. "Jonas, come take a look at this!"

Jonas stepped back into the room with Alicia draped across his arms. "What is it?"

"This door . . . and all along the wall," Ellis said as she leaned closer for a better look. "There's glass here, too. How would the glass from those outside doors get embedded all the way over here?"

"Wind, perhaps," Jonas offered.

"With this much force?" Ellis shook her head. "Some of these shards are embedded nearly the length of my thumb and almost to the ceiling. What kind of wind would do that?"

It was then that Ellis noticed several dark stains against the wall, beginning at about her shoulder height and widening toward the floor.

"Perhaps we had better move on," Jonas said quietly.

Ellis only nodded. She stepped through the broken doorframe into a long hall. The oak doors that should have been in the frame lay against the opposite side of the hall, their finish dusty and weathered. The hall had sets of double marble columns on both sides rising up to support arches that extended down the hall nearly a hundred feet. The patterns of French blue and white tiles could barely be seen beneath the layer of dust under her feet. Dull light from the morning gave scarce illumination through the dirty, round windows set on the far side. The bottom of a wide, marble staircase rose up from the hallway to Ellis's left while the hall ended in a closed door at the far end and a crossing hall behind her.

Jonas stepped through the door, lowering Alicia's feet so that she might stand on her own. He spoke with some assurance. "I remember this hall."

"Which way, then?" Ellis asked.

"The stairs, I think," Jonas answered.

"You *think*?" Ellis looked sharply at the man with the paisley-shaped blemish across his right eye and face. "Aren't you *sure*?"

"It's the Tween, Ellis," Jonas replied, hurt coloring his tone. "It's always changing and being changed. One can never be *sure* about anything, but I do know how to find Jenny."

"And we'll never get out without her," Ellis repeated as though the refrain had become wearily familiar. She absently took her hat off her head and started down the hall with Alicia at her heels following a pace behind Jonas.

They were nearly halfway up the stairs before Ellis noticed them. Two young men in clean dark suits, their collars stiff and starched, tripping down the stairs and engaged in quiet, intense conversation. Their slicked hair gleamed in the light from a broken section of the ceiling overhead. One of them turned his dark eyes to Ellis, half raising his hand in acknowledgment as he smiled.

"Good morning, Ellis!" the young man said in a clear voice.

"Good morning, Murray," Ellis answered easily, and then stopped on the stairs.

Murray turned again to continue his conversation with

his companion as they reached the bottom of the stairs and turned to the left, vanishing from view.

"Who was that?" Alicia asked. "I don't think I've ever seen them before."

"Murray Abramowitz," Ellis said. "He was a fellow student of mine at Boston Medical College."

"Do you think he can help us?" Alicia started down the stairs.

Ellis gripped her shoulder and held her back. "I don't think so, Alicia."

"Why ever not?"

"Because he died in 1914," Ellis said, her brows furrowed as she tried to consider the event. "He was in France at the time."

"War casualty, then?" Jonas asked.

"No," Ellis continued, her voice thoughtful as she spoke. "He was a medical corpsman and was going to war, but it was the flu that took him."

Ellis realized that Jonas was staring at her.

"What is it, Jonas?" Ellis asked.

"You remembered him," Jonas said.

"Yes, I suppose I did," Ellis realized. "But why him? Why Murray Abramowitz? I barely knew the man's name. He was a fellow medical student and I remember the sad irony of his death but he was nothing special to me. Why remember him of all people?"

"Maybe it's easier to remember people who aren't important," Alicia suggested. "They can't hurt you."

Ellis caught her breath before she spoke. "I'm not all that sure I want to remember now."

"Let's keep moving," Jonas urged.

They came to the top of the stairs. The landing there was absent of any furniture or ornamentation. There was a pair of doors opposite the staircase with more doors to the right and left. The ceiling was a dome of stained glass through which scant light shone down.

Ellis looked at Jonas.

"To the right," he said, "I think."

"Aren't you sure?"

"A great many of the corridors are duplicates," Jonas replied. "Knowing where you are isn't a question of which corridor you're in, so much as which similar corridor is connected to which other similar corridor and in what order. Let me take a quick look around a couple of corners to be certain. Wait here."

Jonas moved to the corridor to their right, slipping quickly out of view.

"Corridors on top of corridors," Alicia huffed. "I'm sure I don't know why he insists on using the passageways. The larger rooms should afford us faster progress and they are all connecting."

"I take it you've been in this part of the house, too?" Ellis asked.

"Oh, certainly! Although I'll admit to it being such a very long time ago. Since before you left, in fact. Merrick was so determined to be rid of any remembrance of you that he sealed this Book and had vowed never to open it again. Of course, that was before you . . ." Alicia paused, looking around her in alarm. "Did you hear that?"

"Hear what?"

"That sound," Alicia whispered. "Listen!"

Soft sobbing. It echoed slightly but sounded quite nearby.

"Through there," Alicia murmured, her hand pointing toward one of the doors opposite the stairs leading to the landing.

Ellis stepped toward one of the doors. It was slightly ajar. She gave it a gentle push and it opened onto a large assembly room, towering nearly two stories high to a recessed ceiling. The paint was fading but Ellis could see that the walls had been decorated to look as though they had Roman columns with ornamental garlands between them. Plaques with Roman inscriptions were also painted onto the walls and the ceiling featured Baroque paintings as well. There were arched doors leading out of the room on both sides and a second set of arched doors at the far end of the assembly room. The far doors were open to a dark crossing corridor beyond.

A small face peered back at Ellis through the left-hand door at the far opposite side of the room. It was the face of a girl—perhaps eight or so years old. Her hair was carefully braided with bright red bows matching her dress.

The girl stepped quickly back, her visage vanishing from the open doorway.

"Hello?" Ellis offered, her voice echoing between the fading, stained walls of the assembly room.

"What is it, Ellis?" Alicia asked behind her.

The face of the little girl appeared again. She stepped out to stand in the archway. She didn't move, just stared back at Ellis, wet streaks of tears running down both of her cheeks.

"I don't know," Ellis said to Alicia. She turned her attention to the girl. "Don't be afraid, little one. I'll help you. Are you lost?"

Ellis stepped into the room, her quick strides carrying her across the floor. The floor groaned with every step. She could feel the soft boards, spongy and weak, giving beneath her footfalls.

"Ellis!" Jonas had appeared at the door behind her, calling out. "Wait!"

She took another step toward the little girl.

A great crack resounded through the room as the floorboards gave way beneath her.

Ellis fell through the rotted floor.

11

HIDE & SEEK

A mold-ridden couch collapsed beneath Ellis, breaking her fall as she crashed down onto it from the room above. Instinctively, she held her forearms in front of her face, her eyes held tightly shut. She felt the floorboards, strips of wooden lathe slats and a cloud of crumbling plaster rain down about her.

"Ellis!" She could hear Jonas call desperately down for her from somewhere above. "Are you all right?"

She held her breath, daring not to move until the debris had settled.

"Ellis!" Jonas called more anxiously. "Please! Answer me! Are you hurt?"

"Only my pride, I think," Ellis responded.

Ellis tentatively shifted her arms, venturing to open one eye. The plaster dust still hung in the air but there was sufficient light from the hole in the ceiling to see the extent of the room. It was nearly a match in size to the one above it although in this case its walls were wainscoted with dull, gilded edges. There were a number of furniture pieces in the room, a second couch and several chairs. The upholstery on each was swollen and the stuffing bulging outward from tears in the fabric. It appeared to Ellis to be some kind of sitting room or antechamber, although to what she could not guess. The arrangement of the rooms in this place was still baffling and without any reason that she could fathom.

Ellis moved with deliberate caution as she sat up. She looked up and was surprised to see that the ceiling was over fifteen feet above her. The anxious faces of Alicia and Jonas were staring back at her, silhouetted against the light from the dome of the room above.

Ellis brushed the splintered wood off of her traveling suit, her legs still slightly uncertain as she stood up. "What about the girl? Is she still there?"

"What girl?" Jonas asked.

"There was a little girl on the far side of the . . . oh, never mind." Ellis could see from the expression on Jonas's face that if there were any little girl in the doorway before she was most certainly not there now. "I seem to have taken a detour."

"We'll get you out in a minute, Ellis," Alicia said, her voice wavering slightly, betraying her uncertainty.

"I don't see how." Ellis shook her head. "Unless either

of you have been carrying a ladder or even just a good
length of rope that I don't know about."

"Listen. I've found a long gallery up here that should
keep us ahead of Merrick," Jonas called down to her from
the ruined ceiling above her.

"And what happens if he catches up with us?" Ellis
asked.

"Just stay where you are"—Jonas had already vanished
from the hole, his voice distant and echoing—"and I'll
find a way to get you out."

"Don't worry, Ellis," her father said to her. "It's just a game."
Ellis shivered. The memories of her past kept bubbling
up into her conscious mind. They were not complete:
only phrases or lines from people whom she suddenly
cared for deeply and yet, at the same time, still felt removed from. It was like a badly scratched phonograph
record that would play a few notes of a familiar song and
then skip entirely to a completely different tune.

She concentrated on the room, trying to keep the
memories at bay for the time being. Like the room above,
there were six exits from the room—one at each side of
the end walls and one in the center of each of the longer
sides—although here the oak doors with the dull finish
were all shut. There were paintings mounted to the walls
above the wainscot in a patchwork of frames that encir-
cled the room. Each lay in shadow with no light shining
directly on their canvases.

Ellis took a step closer to one of the longer walls,

peering intently at the largest of the paintings there as she approached it.

She stopped.

It was a depiction of the Curtis lighthouse during a storm. The waves crashed against the island's eastern rocks, rising up and seeming to engulf the structure. The lighthouse stood against the threatening darkness, its beam cast outward through the rain and over the sea. Two small figures could be seen silhouetted against the lamp: a woman and a small child both clinging to the railing and threatened by the storm.

Ellis shifted her gaze to another, smaller piece of art next to it. This depicted a nursery with a bassinet near a window but there was something wrong in the composition of the painting. The light coming through the glass illuminated an empty rocking chair in stark light while casting the more prominent cradle in shadow. Beyond the glass was a bright garden with a picket fence and a gate.

Ellis looked closer.

There, beyond the gate, was the shadowed figure of a man.

"Jenny!"

The name echoed, as though being summoned from a distance.

Above her, Alicia gasped.

It sounded as though it came from the direction where Ellis thought the stairs might be.

"Jenny!"

Ellis spun to her left. It was a deeper voice calling this time and closer from beyond the long wall on her left.

"Oh, Ellis," Alicia said, her voice now tightened to a fearful squeak. "They're getting closer!"

"Quiet!" Ellis called up in hushed tones. "Where's Jonas?"

"I don't know!" Alicia looked about her, her voice quivering. "He left . . . I don't know where he went!"

"Jenny!"

"Jenny!"

"Jen-ny!"

Multiple voices this time. Ellis thought they were coming from the end of the room that would have been back toward the staircase.

The voices were getting closer.

"You've got to run!" Alicia whispered hoarsely from above.

"Why?" Ellis asked, her eyes fixed on the closed doors at the end of the hall directly beneath where Alicia stared down at her. "They're looking for Jenny, not me. We're *all* looking for Jenny!"

"It doesn't matter," Alicia called desperately back at her. "After what you did to Merrick's play, running like that from the theater . . . if they catch you, there's no telling what he'll do to you!"

A sudden knocking shook the door behind Ellis.

She jumped at the sound, turning. She waited a

moment but nothing happened. She took a step toward the door.

"Ellis!" Alicia whispered frantically from above. "Don't open it!"

Ellis glanced up. "Maybe it's Jonas."

Silence filled the space for a moment. Ellis reached hesitantly for the stained brass doorknob.

"Run," Alicia whimpered. "Oh, please, just run."

A thunderous knocking shook the door in front of her so violently that she could see the upper corner separate from the frame.

Ellis jumped back, turned and ran.

She ran for the far end of the room, twisting the doorknob and throwing open the door. The hall she entered twisted mazelike deeper into the ruins. The doors to either side were open as she fled down the corridor, weak light streaming in from each one as she rushed past. There were voices coming from the rooms as well, echoing in the abandoned space. Sometimes muffled and sometimes entirely too clear.

"*That is a completely inappropriate question for Sunday School, Sister Harkington! I shall speak to your mother about this immediately after . . .*"

"*From what lurid magazine did you copy this story, young lady? Ellis, do not deny it! You could not possibly have written anything this well on your own . . .*"

"*She's a Harkington! No one who is anyone speaks to the Harkingtons. They're such a disgrace . . .*"

"Gee, Ellis, I'd really like to take you to the dance but there's this other girl . . ."

Out of the corner of her eye, she could see dark, shadowy figures standing in the rooms but she kept running. The memories each voice sparked were painful, vivid and, worst of all, entirely her own. Each incident rushed up into her mind with painful awareness. The Minister's Wife, the Teacher, the Girls from her class, the Boy in the empty classroom; each memory with its disappointments, pain and shame rushed at her out of each open doorway like a terrible jack-in-the-box of the mind, springing hurtful memories at her from her childhood.

Ellis steeled herself against them, running faster down the twisting gauntlet of her childhood.

Other voices, too, were still heard behind her.

"Jenny!" they called like hounds at her heels. *"Come out, come out, wherever you are!"*

The hallway abruptly ended at a door. She pulled it open with vehemence, charging into the room beyond.

She nearly collided with the broken bed in the corner of the room. Rebecca, her childhood friend when Ellis was only eight years old, lay in it coughing weakly and covered in the measles. She reached out her blotched hand for Ellis, calling her name. Ellis swept quickly past the bed to the next door beyond, forcing it open with her shoulder.

She stumbled onto a landing at the top of a steep, spiraling set of stairs. Ellis went right instead, following the corner to a short hall on the left. She was running now as much from the memories as from the baying voices still calling for Jenny.

At least the calling voices seemed to be receding and she thought wildly for a moment that she might have a chance of losing them in the Ruins. Perhaps she could find a place to hide, catch her bearings and perhaps find her way back to Jonas and Alicia.

The hallway ended at another door. A ball that Ellis had lost when she was three lay in the corner. She willed herself to ignore it and pressed on through the doorway.

Ellis stopped abruptly on the other side.

Snow was gently falling beyond the tall windows on the far side of the room. The polished, sumptuous oak paneling was practically aglow from the warm light of the fire raging in the large, marble fireplace to one side. Opposite the fireplace and set in one corner of the room, an enormous evergreen tree stood decorated in bows, strings of popcorn and berries as well as paper ornaments and candles.

Candles her papa had lit for her.

Ellis drew in a shuddering breath.

There he sat, her father in his favorite wingback chair.

He was too plump and his cheeks were, perhaps, a little too rosy. He was still wearing his tuxedo slacks but he had draped his coat over the back of the couch that sat opposite him and had opened the front of his vest. The tie was nowhere to be seen. He had even somehow managed to be rid of his polished shoes, favoring instead his tattered and far more comfortable slippers. He sat with his legs outstretched, crossed at the feet, and peered at a book he held in his hands.

He looked up and saw her.

He smiled.

He closed the book and held his arms out wide to her just as he had when she was fifteen years old. Her mother was still out at the Cabots' party trying to get the support of Elise Cabot for Mother's latest social project. Papa had managed to slip away early and take refuge in the parlor. Ellis had heard him and come down from her room, far too excited on Christmas Eve to sleep.

"You're still up, my girl?" His voice was warm and welcoming, as familiar to her as anything could be. The joy in its memory wounded her heart with longing. "Come on, my girl! Give me my present early! A little hug for your old father, eh? How about a story?"

How could she have forgotten this night? She had carried it with her down through the years, a precious moment of her own never to share, never to lose. The silent snow falling outside and only the crackle of the fire to disturb them. He had lit all the candles on the tree for them—just for them alone—and then they had settled into that great chair together, her in her father's lap with his left arm cradling her and his right hand steadying the book. It was Dickens's *A Christmas Carol* and, with her mother away for the evening, her father did not skip over the ghostly parts but performed them with relish for his appreciative audience of one. Curled up on his lap, it was the safest she had ever felt or would ever feel. It was the memory she recalled when nothing else could bring her peace.

Ellis stepped across the room, tears welling up in her eyes. She fell to her knees next to him, throwing her arms around her papa's waist and resting her head against his chest just as she had those many years ago.

"Oh, Papa," she sobbed. "I've missed you so!"

"There, there, my dear girl," her father said. His hand began to stroke her hair. "It's Christmas! Everything is just fine. Your mother will be at the Cabots' a while longer. Let's have some time of our own."

"The Cabots'?" Ellis chuckled through her tears. "And this is good old Boston . . ."

Her papa grinned down at her. He had been at the dinner in 1910 and heard the toast himself. That he had taught it to their daughter was a source of never-ending grief for her mother. He dutifully delivered the next line. "The home of the bean and the cod. Where the Lowells talk only to Cabots . . ."

They finished the toast together.

"And the Cabots talk only to God."

They laughed heartily together, then, overcome, Ellis once again buried her face against her father's open vest, breathing in the smell of his clothes and his pipe tobacco.

She took no notice of the voices approaching beyond the walls.

Ellis closed her eyes. "Please read to me, Papa."

"Of course, my girl!"

"And do all the voices," she said.

"I always do all the voices," came the deeper, darker-sounding voice of her father behind her.

She opened her eyes wide.

The floorboards in the room were rotting through in places. The oak paneling was warped and cracking from neglect. The tree was entirely gone but the old wingback chair remained, its fabric torn and stuffing exploding outward from the holes.

Her father was gone.

She leaped upward, trying to run, but a strong hand gripped her wrist and spun her around. She tried to strike the face that was suddenly before her with her free hand but he managed to grip that, too, pulling both her hands back behind her as he held her close.

"You left my party too soon," Merrick said, staring down at her with his pain-filled eyes. "You owe me a dance, Ellis. You most definitely owe me a dance."

12

THE WALTZ

Merrick dragged her away from the rotting wing-back chair, pushing through a door beyond the bookcase. Ellis glimpsed the books as she passed, each with a faded spine and no title. She wondered if they, too, were fake or whether they were filled with words entombed between their covers, never to be read—never to live.

"So you want the past?" Merrick sneered as he pulled her into the hallway. "Nostalgia, is it? A longing for those memories of the good old days? How fortunate to be so selective, so discerning about our own past that we can pick and choose that which justifies who we have become."

The hall ended in an enormous foyer with curved staircases rising on either side to a landing above. The ceiling frescoes were largely fallen to plaster rubble on the ground, though here and there the original square pattern could be seen still intact. The stair treads looked as precarious as the floor she had fallen through earlier but there was light coming from beyond the landing.

Merrick began pulling her up the left-hand stairs. The treads and stringers swayed under their weight.

"Let go of me!" Ellis yelled, her struggles powerless against his iron grip.

"After all I've done for you." Merrick's voice shook as though he were about to sob. "After all I've built to protect you. Why can't you just let it all go as we have? Why do you insist on this futile pursuit of an answer that you really do not wish to know?"

"Is that why you hid Jenny from me?" Ellis demanded. "Because she's known the truth all along?"

"Here you are looking for all the answers in your cousin Jenny," Merrick laughed. They were at the top of the stairs where a set of doors shone with light through the dust coating the panes. "That would be funny indeed if it were not so sad."

Ellis could hear the first strains of music coming from beyond the doors, the sounds of an orchestra tuning up.

"So you want to know your past?" Merrick asked. His bright eyes seemed to burn as he looked down at her, standing far too close for her comfort. "Then, by all means let me grant your wish."

He reached over to the stained bronze handle of the

door, pushing her through before him as he swung it open. A gentle rhythmic plucking of a string was soon joined by a long, soft chorus of violins.

There was nothing but the music beyond the doorway, a waltz she recognized as written by Camille Saint-Saëns.

It was the *Danse Macabre*.

Her body began to disintegrate as she spun into the nothingness. The drab, green skirt, the jacket, blouse, hat, shoes, stockings—everything dissolved and whirled away from her as she rotated in a void. She desperately tried to reclaim it, to gather it back in, but the skin of her arms fled from her, too. She tried to scream but her throat and larynx were already gone. They drifted into dust as she revolved to the three-count music of the waltz, their particles followed by her muscles and sinews, tendons, bowels and entrails. Her lungs drifted as dry flecks outward between her ribs and then her bones exploded into the growing mist that surrounded her.

She was thought. She was intelligence. She was entity. All that and nothing more.

The music pressed on about her, spinning her without direction until the mists coalesced about her. Now the spinning of the dance was gathering elements of herself together, but she was not alone, for in the surrounding mists there were others who were gathering as well, taking form out of thought into being. Soon they began to take on shapes she could recognize. Alicia Van der Meer, Ely Rossini, Silenus Tune . . . each of them also spinning to the music near her. As the music continued on, Ellis's apprehension grew at the number of figures forming in the enormous ballroom, each spinning to the music.

She realized with a shock that she was dancing with Merrick.

It was as though she were seeing him for the first time. His features were perfection, as though he were the model for Olympian heroes appearing in its perfect form. He was a bright, shining star smiling down on her.

Through the spinning ghostly spirits that crowded around them, Ellis was astonished that Jonas was spinning toward them. Merrick reached out his hand. In a moment, the three of them were joined in a ring, dancing to the waltz in a circle of chain steps, swinging their arms together in the joy of their common movement and the jubilation at having form and substance. Jonas was now different than he first appeared to Ellis. There was no great paisley discoloration marring his face. He was handsome and his eyes shone as he looked at her.

Together, they moved down the hall. Ellis sensed they were progressing toward the far end but she could not yet see it over the heads of the souls whirling about her.

Then the music changed. It became discordant and mellow. A violin struck down on the strings with discord and the music took a darker and more combative turn. The spinning dancers began to separate to the left and the right of the hall. Jonas, Merrick and Ellis spun faster and faster to the music, being pulled one way or the other.

Merrick and Jonas argued with each other though Ellis could not hear their words over the music filling the ballroom.

Jonas angrily let go of Merrick's hand. The circle of the three friends was suddenly unbalanced and they stumbled in the dance. Jonas clung to Ellis's hand but something inside of her feared that the dance would end.

Ellis knew that this had all happened before.

Ellis let go of Jonas's hand.

The young man spun off to the side, his face contorted in pain and disappointment as Merrick quickly closed the waltz frame with Ellis and they spun together down the center of the hall. Alicia, Silenus, Ely and all the members of the Nightbirds Society were dancing about them, spinning down the ballroom. By then, all the people of Gamin had joined them. Other voices from the sides of the room called to them, beckoning them to follow them into the salons on either side of the dance floor, but the music played on and still Merrick and Ellis continued their mad dance down the interminable ballroom.

The room itself began to change and Ellis changed with it. Merrick held her in a firm waltz pose as they spun to the sound of the orchestra still filling the room but now he was dressed in a Greek chiton off one shoulder with a laurel wreath encircling his head. Ellis realized with a shock that she wore a Doric chiton, her hair in a complex style reminiscent of those she had once seen on Grecian urns. The ballroom had suddenly evolved into Doric

columns. Around them, the rest of the citizens she recognized as coming from Gamin were spinning about them in
more common costumes. Ellis and Merrick were the
rulers of this domain, the center of the dance about which
everyone else orbited.

In an instant it all shifted again. Merrick was in a regal
coat with a ruff at his neck, his hair suddenly a powdered
wig. Ellis realized that she was now in a long ball gown.
Her hair was piled high upon her head, held in place by
a gaudy tiara. The hall, too, had changed, its architecture now more Baroque and gilded. Still, Alicia, Silenus,
Ely and the others from the town continued to whirl
about her.

Ellis searched desperately beyond the faces of the dancers spinning about her. Everyone familiar to her had
departed the dance floor except for Jonas. He moved at
the very edge of the hall, his eyes on Ellis, as though waiting for something.

Merrick spun her suddenly beneath his arm, then took
her again firmly in his hold.

"I made you a queen here," Merrick whispered in her
ear over the driving rhythm of the music. "Anything you
wished became the heart of our Game. Anyone who offended you was punished. Anyone who pleased you was
rewarded. It was me that you followed. I was the only
choice you made . . ."

The hall shifted again and retook the shape of the ballroom but this time it was no longer a ruin. The fallen

plaster at the corners rose up to the ceiling to retake its place. The paint erupted in luster and the gilding took on its former glow. The dusty chandeliers shook off the years, the spent wax rising up to reform their candles, each of which erupted again with flame and light. Merrick was impeccably dressed in a morning coat, waistcoat, and formal striped trousers. Ellis glanced down at her own dress, a beautiful formal gown with a wide skirt flaring out with their every turn.

She gazed up into his eyes.

They were dark, cold, filled with hunger but no passion.

"We were together, Ellis." Merrick's smile was chilling. "We could be again."

Ellis pulled her right hand away from Merrick's shoulder, lifting her left, and she turned under him. It was a simple pivot but as she turned she let go completely of his right hand, spinning away from him intentionally.

In an instant, Jonas stepped in, grasped her again in his hold and continued the dance. Somehow her dress was caught under Merrick's foot and Jonas pulling her away ripped the dress, leaving a huge patch of the cloth behind as the skirt of the ball gown shredded and tore away.

The wheeling dance continued but it was not the same. The ballroom floor was suddenly packed with souls she did not recognize, separating her from Merrick, Alicia and the rest of the Gamin crowd who now were only at the farthest fringes of the floor. The music had become more desperate and driving, darker, faster in tempo and more sinister.

"Hold on to me, Ellis," Jonas pleaded, his eyes welling up with tears. "You must stay with me until the end of the dance. No matter what happens . . . we must finish this dance!"

The changes around them were happening more quickly now. They were whirling through the Boston Common, a grotto in the midst of the city where Jonas had knelt before her with as expensive a ring as he could manage.

Then they were dancing at their wedding. There was her mother glaring her disapproval from the side of the room. Then the dance was suddenly unbearably crowded in the small apartment that was a secret disappointment to her though Jonas was showing it to her with such pride.

"Hold on, Ellis," Jonas begged. "Please, hold on."

The dance turned more violent. It seemed more of a tango now than a waltz although the music drove on as before. She was dancing around Jonas in one of the few dresses she could still wear to her medical studies. Jonas wore rougher clothing, too. His face was no longer cleanly shaven, his hair was unkempt and his face flushed. He would stop her in her dance, twist her about violently into a new pose. Their contact became rough and their dance steps sharp and staccato in nature. His eyes were bleary as he gazed more through her than at her.

Ellis let go of Jonas, turning away from him on the floor.

The dancers in the hall stopped.

The music suddenly changed. An oboe sounded a set of notes, followed by violins in a low, minor key tremolo.

Ellis was once again in her dull, green traveling suit. She took a step backward away from Jonas.

"Please," he begged through watery, red-rimmed eyes. He held his hand out toward her even as he staggered uncertainly before her. "Not now! We have to finish the dance!"

Ellis hesitated.

"My lady!"

Ellis turned toward the sound.

"Don't trust them." Margaret was running toward her from a side door into the ballroom. She grabbed Ellis's hand, pulling her back toward the door. "It's all a trap. They'll keep you here forever if you stay!"

Ellis fled the ballroom with Margaret.

"No!" howled Jonas.

Ellis slammed the doors of the ballroom closed behind her. Margaret was already far ahead of her, still running down the tall gallery of paintings that looked as though it might never end. Ellis ran after her, calling down the hall as she passed the portraits, "Margaret, wait!"

Margaret slowed her steps as Ellis caught up to her.

Ellis dared not look at the faces from the paintings; she could feel their eyes following her as she passed them.

"Where are you taking me, Margaret?" Ellis demanded.

"To where you can get your answers," Margaret replied. "To those who know everything that ever was or will ever be."

"Then show me," Ellis said.

The waltz played on behind them as they fled down the gallery.

●

13

A SPOT OF TEA

The drawing room was falling apart. The floorboards were warped and the painted plaster on the walls was crumbling. The patterns on what little wallpaper remained merged with dreadful stains. Several of the panes of glass in the tall arched windows were missing while the rest barely permitted the light to penetrate let alone afforded a view of the dead garden beyond.

In the center of the room was a round claw-foot table leaning precariously to one side. It was covered in a ragged and stained satin spread with tattered, yellowing lace on top of it. A lazy Susan sat precariously in the middle of the slanting tabletop, an assortment of creamers, sugar bowls and a prominent china teapot all covered in dust and linked by cobwebs. A cart sat to one side, its plates each covered with molding cake.

Ellis sat on one side of the table. Margaret stood just behind Ellis's chair, her hands folded primly in front of her as she waited.

In the remaining seats around the circular table, the three Disir sisters sat in faded and threadbare dresses and tattered blouses. Each wore a corsage of brittle, dead flowers pinned to the collar of their quaintly unfashionable Zouave jackets.

Minnie leaned forward, pouring a tea flecked with dregs into the chipped cups. Not a trace of steam escaped from the liquid. Ellis assumed it had gone cold.

"Don't you just love antiques?" Minnie gushed.

"I assume you are referring to the furniture and not the company?" sniffed Finny.

Margaret spoke before Ellis had a moment to reply. "It was so good of you to receive her ladyship on such short notice."

"It is our honor to receive your call," said Linny Disir, although the tone of her voice was devoid of the warmth her words implied. Linny picked up a needlepoint frame and began working the thread at once. "We seldom have guests in this part of the house. Still we keep ourselves busy."

"Busy, indeed!" chirped Minnie.

"Please, I need your help," Ellis said quickly before Margaret could interrupt again.

"*You* need *our* help?" Finny scoffed. "Now that *is* amusing, is it not, sisters?"

"Most amusing," Linny said without a trace of a smile.

"May I offer you some cake?" Minnie said cheerfully as she gestured toward the cart.

Ellis glanced at the mold bloom that completely obscured the cake slices. "No, thank you, Miss Minnie. Please, I need you to tell me where to find Jenny."

The Disir sisters looked at each other in surprise.

"Merrick has hidden her somewhere in the house," Ellis pressed on. "I need to find her if I'm ever going to leave again."

"But it's *your* house," Linny observed with a puzzled expression on her face. "You, above anyone else, ought to be able to remember where to find her."

"But I don't remember," Ellis said. "At least, I don't remember this house."

"You don't remember anything?" Finny asked as her eyes narrowed in suspicion.

"Not about here. I do remember a few things about my life in Boston," Ellis replied. "Bits and fragments of family or people or events, but they're all like a handful of pieces from a jigsaw puzzle, none of which seem to fit together and certainly did not seem to be enough to complete the entire picture."

"Will someone please remind me about Boston?" Linny asked.

"Well, not that I know anything about it," piped up Minnie, "but I understand that it is a big city where Ellis grew up as a child and then met and married—oh, what's his name?"

"Jonas." Finny frowned. "Jonas Kirk."

"Yes, that's the name," Minnie chirped happily at the prompt. "Of course they weren't always in Boston and he treated her rather badly when they lost that child but then I suppose that's the way of the world, so I hear. I remember—and you can back me up on this Finny as I recall remarking on it at the time—that it was a real shame considering that it was he who coerced Ellis through the Gate in the first place—"

"Mind your tongue, Minnie!" Finny scolded. "You know the rules to the Game!"

"Oh, piffle to the rules," Minnie sniffed.

"Merrick was most specific when he sent me to bring her back on the train," Finny said, her tight dark curls bouncing slightly in her sudden rage. "We were not to discuss her past with Ellis, especially the time before she left us."

"Well, if there is anything that I *do* know," Minnie groused back at her sister, "it is that those were the rules to the old Game. That Book is closed and now we're back to playing *this* Game. We are in Echo House again and there are no such rules here!"

"Minnie is correct," Linny interjected, the tone of her voice daring anyone to question her ruling on the subject. "This Game is an old Book and its rules have not been altered by Merrick. There is no prohibition against talking of Ellis's past in these rules."

"You can't win the game until you know the rules . . ." her *mother had said.*

"So the rules of this Game are different from those in Gamin?" Ellis said more as a question than a statement.

"Each Day has its rules," Finny said as though she were stating the obvious.

"You mean they change at sunset or midnight or . . ."

"Nonsense, child," Finny sniffed. "I'm not talking about *that* kind of day. I mean the Day, as in the Day in which we live. Whoever wins the Game rules the new Day and their Book becomes the rules for the next Game."

"Not that I know anything about it." Minnie was anxious to take a larger part in the conversation. "But each Book has a different set of rules for the Day according to the life each soul would like to live. Absolutely everyone here in the Tween seems to have a Book of their own Day . . . the Day that they would like to pretend at living."

"Not everyone." Linny gave an exasperated sigh.

"No, of course, not *everyone,*" Minnie corrected. "The Outsiders never do—Soldiers or Shades for example—but they come from beyond the Tween. They're always trying to persuade us to leave and take sides in the Great War but they have nothing to do with the Tween itself. They do seem interested in our Books but none of them have any Books of their own."

"And *we* have no Books of our own nor are we likely ever to have," Finny interrupted her sister. "Neither me nor either of my sisters have any desires toward winning the Day. We're all perfectly content living in other people's lives. It's so much easier to play in other people's dreams than making all that effort to create dreams of our own. We're content to live by the rules of other people's Days."

"Then this house has its own set of laws . . . its own rules," Ellis said as much to herself as the sisters. "Who made them?"

Minnie beamed a smile over her dead corsage. "Why, *you* did, my dear!"

"Me?" Ellis exclaimed.

"Echo House was your Book," Linny said, her broad face turned directly toward Ellis. "You made this place."

"*I* made this place?" Ellis sounded incredulous.

"Perhaps a cucumber sandwich?" Minnie's offering was nearly overgrown with mold.

"No, thank you! How is this possible?" Ellis asked. "I don't remember anything about this mad place!"

"But of course you wouldn't," snapped Finny, setting down her own needlepoint. "That's the way of the world, isn't it? You leave this place and forget about us entirely. Off you go beyond the Gate without so much as a thank-you or fare-thee-well!"

"Who was I?" Ellis asked, dreading the answer. "Who was I before . . . before the Gate?"

"You were royalty here in those days," Minnie gushed.

"Merrick made the first Day for you. Of course, I don't know that much about it but—"

"Begging your pardon, ladies," Margaret interrupted the sisters. "I believe you must begin further back than that. May I suggest you start with Merrick, Jonas and Ellis?"

"Oh, yes," Minnie beamed. "Quite right!"

"Merrick, Jonas and me?" Ellis asked.

"Oh, let me tell!" Minnie begged.

"I'll tell it," Finny interrupted. "You may know where to start but you'll never know when to stop."

"No, sisters," Linny said firmly. "I'll tell the tale."

The other two sisters quieted at once. Ellis turned toward Linny.

"Once before a time," Linny began, "there were three great souls who awoke in the heavens. There were, of course, legions of others but these three came to know and love each other. Two were of men and one was of woman. They were inseparable friends. Each was beautiful and clever in their own way and together they were incomparably glorious."

"And they were?" Ellis urged softly.

"We'll call them Merrick, Jonas and Ellis," Finny said. "They each took great joy in their awakening and in the companionship of each other. The challenge of differing thoughts and perspectives was compelling for them."

"But it didn't last," Minnie burst out breathlessly. "There came the moment—"

"Minnie!" Linny said sharply.

Her sister quieted at once.

Linny breathed in and continued. "But there came a moment when all the gathered souls had to choose for themselves which of two brothers they would follow. A new world, a new creation had been formed but one brother proposed one Book and the other proposed another for its founding rules. Some followed one, some followed the other. This was the choice that every soul was asked to make."

"Tragedies have such hopeful beginnings," Minnie sighed.

"This choice broke the friendship of these three spirits. Jonas had chosen to follow one of the two brothers, but his love for you was a powerful bond. Merrick wanted you for himself. He did not care to choose at all. He was not persuaded by the promises of either of the brothers."

"And between the two brothers," Ellis asked, though she felt a chill up her spine, "which did I choose?"

A thin smile formed on Linny's face. "You, my dear, chose Merrick."

Ellis shuddered.

"Oh, you were such a grand couple," Minnie gushed. "Even in our banishment."

"This was the place provided for us," Linny continued in quiet reminiscence. "A place far from creation. A place beyond heaven. A place beyond hell. It was you who named it the 'Tween' and, with Merrick, helped to create the first Game . . . it sprang from your Book. You established rules after the pattern of the First Parents . . . important rules like up and down, light and dark, ground and air and liquid. It was all imagined, of course, since no one had any real experience with that sort of thing. Everyone who followed Merrick here depended on you both to establish the rules of the Day. Of course, there were the unbreakable rules, but you managed to forge a credible dream of existence within their strictures."

"Unbreakable rules?" Ellis pressed. "What are the unbreakable rules?"

"The rules that forged this existence," Finny replied. "Haven't you been paying attention? The rules of the Great War."

"Perhaps you would like a biscuit?" Minnie offered. "You're looking a bit pale."

"I'm sorry." Ellis shook her head, trying to understand. "The Great War . . . the war in Europe?"

"Oh, nonsense, child!" Finny huffed. "The Great War of Spirits! The war between the two brothers for the souls of creation!"

"The governing rules of the formation of the Tween require the Gates in every Book of the Day," Linny continued, her cold stare daring either of her sisters to interrupt her again.

"You said Gates." Ellis leaned forward against the table, causing it to creak ominously. "There are more than one, then?"

"Oh, yes." Linny nodded. "There are at least two of which we know. One is guarded by a creature called Uriel. We believe he, too, is a Soldier, for that is the Gate from which the Soldiers come. The other is watched over by a different creature we only know as Belial. Through them occasionally come warriors of the Great War to try and persuade one of us to choose at last between the brothers and thereby pass back through the Gate with them. The existence of these Gates—and an avenue of access to them—is a founding rule of the Tween and cannot be violated."

"But it is often made very difficult," Minnie added. "Merrick has gotten very clever at hiding them."

"These warriors who came through the Gates were a nuisance but the Soldiers that came through Uriel's Gate brought an unexpected boon—each of them had lived a mortal life before they came among us. You, Ellis, were the first to learn this from them and with that knowledge you began creating Books of the Day that were dreams very much like the mortal world."

"That's when you built this house, my lady," Margaret said from behind her. "There had never been anything like it before."

"Oh, my, yes! Not that I know anything about it, mind

you," Minnie cheerfully gushed. "But Merrick learned so much from you and, oh, what amazing Days were to be had! At first, different people were able to take control of the Days with their own Books but it was very quickly a battle between you and Merrick as to who could beat each other at their Day. It was a wonderful time with everyone wondering what new dark delight you would come up with for each new Day."

"That is until you ruined it," Finny groused.

"Ruined it?" Ellis exclaimed. "How?"

"You broke the rules, that's how," Finny snapped back. "Somehow you cheated and broke the rules—the rules of the Gate of all things! All for that Jonas boy! All for a *Soldier,* of all the thoughtless . . ."

Linny put her long-fingered hand on Finny's arm. Finny glanced at her sister and then slowly settled back into her chair.

"They'll be coming soon," Margaret urged. "We've got to leave, my lady."

"But I have so many more questions," Ellis protested.

"You know everything you need! All you need is Jenny and the Gate," Margaret said quietly at Ellis's ear. "Find a Soldier and you're halfway home. Find Jenny and you can leave all this behind."

"The Soldiers," Ellis said to Linny. "They came in through the Gate so then they must know where the Gate is to go back."

"Must they?" Linny asked.

"Why wouldn't they?"

"I would say"—Linny smiled without humor as she spoke—"that is entirely up to you."

14

DOLLHOUSE

Ellis wanted to run but she held her steps to a quickened pace as she passed out the farthest door of the molding tearoom. The Disir sisters were just as disquieting here as they had been in Gamin—a symmetry that Ellis found reassuring on some deeper level. There was a consistency to the madness in which she moved.

Science is repeatable. Where there is consistency there is an underlying law.

She could not recall the professor's name but she remembered his words clearly. She reminded herself that there were rules to this Game. She needed time . . . time to think through the apparent insanity to find the rules that governed it.

Yet Finny said that she had broken the rules—

supposedly unbreakable rules of the Gate that governed everything here, wherever "here" was or meant.

There is an underlying law . . .

"Which way does your ladyship wish to go?" Margaret demanded as much as asked. Their exit from the room had left them on a landing at the end of a hall that appeared to extend for miles into the distance. Stairs on their left spiraled upward while to their right they spiraled down.

"What?" Ellis remained distracted by her thoughts. Minnie had said that Merrick had gotten rather good at hiding the Gate and Linny had intimated that whether the Soldiers knew where to find the Gate or not would be largely up to Ellis. The house itself was created by her, if the Disir sisters were to be believed, but how could she possibly have done so? Even if the Gate were hidden from the rest of the souls here, wasn't it a fundamental rule that the Soldiers and demons *had* to be able to find their way out?

"Does your ladyship wish to go upstairs or down?" Margaret repeated, more urgently. "Which way?"

"I don't know," Ellis blurted out in her frustration. She was trying to think and Margaret's badgering kept derailing her thoughts.

"But you're the mistress of the house," Margaret insisted. "It's your Day!"

"My Day or not, I have no idea where to go in this madhouse!" Ellis shouted. It felt good to release the rage and frustration though Margaret shrank from it. "I haven't since I set foot in this place!"

"But I can help you," Margaret suggested meekly. "Just tell me what to do. Anything and I'll do it."

"But I don't know what to do or where to go," Ellis huffed. "*That's* why I needed a guide, Margaret! That's why I followed Jonas."

"Do you want me to fetch him for you?" Margaret said in a quiet, cautious voice. "Do you trust him to lead you through your own house?"

Ellis blinked. *My own house.*

Ever since she had arrived in Echo House, the memories of her past had begun to rise to the surface of her consciousness. But she suddenly realized that it wasn't just the memories themselves that were returning to her. The house itself was memory, each place turning like the terrible waltz to form meaning out of its very walls.

"I didn't just create the house," Ellis murmured in sudden, terrible wonder. "I'm still creating it."

"Your ladyship?" Margaret asked, her voice still hushed.

"How is that possible?" Ellis said as much to herself as to her companion. She turned about on the landing, looking at the stairs and the long hallway as though they were new to her eyes. "Is this still my Day?"

"No, my lady," Margaret said, shaking her head. "It is Merrick's Day."

"And yet the house is changing to suit me," Ellis said.

"Do you still wish me to fetch Jonas for you, my lady?" Margaret asked.

"No!" Ellis turned a sharp eye toward Margaret. The memory of the last moments of the waltz was still with her. The pain of the memory and the betrayal of her trust in him remained keen in her mind. "But we do need to find a Soldier."

"Wherever shall we find one?" Margaret asked with a slight quiver in her voice. "They are such frightful things and Merrick said that they had been put away in the furthest reaches of the house."

"Margaret, there must be a way to . . . wait!" Ellis held up her hand. "Did you hear that?"

"I heard nothing, my lady," Margaret replied.

"Quiet, Margaret," Ellis insisted. "Just listen!"

It was in the distance above them. It echoed down the stairwell and was muffled but the sound was light and bubbling.

A laugh.

A child's laugh.

"Come on!" Ellis said even as she rushed up the stairs. She could hear the hard soles of Margaret's ankle boots pounding up the stairs behind her.

The banister of stained wood had a deep red hue to it as though it were made of cherry. As she arrived at the upper landing she could see that the walls were covered in a bottle-green wallpaper that had since faded closer to sage in color. There was a skylight overhead that had just begun to rattle under a fresh rain, making the sound of pebbles tossed against the glass. The lightning flashes were still far off as was, also, the distant rumble of thunder. There was a stained glass window on the right side of the landing, the distant flashes of lightning illuminating the glass sailing ship on a storm-tossed sea. A second window at the head of the stairs was a double-hung window that was partially open. It was the kind of window that was typical of the exterior of a home but when Ellis glanced through it, she saw that it only looked into another room. It was a completely insane choice of placement but, as she reminded herself, what in this house was sane?

The high-pitched laugh was closer now, a bubbling sort of bright laughter coming from just down the short hall with warped floorboards and the same dull sage wallpaper curling away from the walls. Another double-hung window was at the end of the hall, rain now running in rivulets down its surface. There were two paneled doors at the end of the hall, both with peeling paint. The door to the right was slightly ajar, a dim, flickering glow coming from that room.

The light, quick laugh came again.

A baby's laugh.

Ellis stopped. Something inside her was screaming at her to run, to turn and walk away from what was ahead of her. She pushed down the fear rising within her and started with careful, soft steps down the hall.

Margaret followed hesitantly. "Your ladyship—"

"Quiet!" Ellis demanded sotto voce.

The warped floorboards creaked and shifted under her boots as Ellis forced her way down the hall. The sounds of a baby's delight were coming from beyond the slightly open door but she could not yet see into the room.

Ellis reached for the tarnished silver doorknob. The door gave way with reluctance. The sounds of the child silenced abruptly. Ellis knew what awaited her but she went in anyway.

"A nursery?" Margaret said as she followed into the room.

Ellis gave a deep sigh. "Yes. My child's nursery."

The shades of the windows were drawn closed, keeping the room in darkness. Only the light from the struggling fire on the hearth illuminated their surroundings.

It was all just as Ellis remembered it. The empty bassinet sitting unused in the corner. The rocking chair sitting in perfect stillness by the fireplace, its shine now dulled by a thin covering of dust. A hamper and a changing table. The wallpaper that she had chosen. She had been so terribly critical of Jonas's handiwork when he first put it up and insisted he redo it to her satisfaction.

All for the child's sake.

Their child's sake.

Her child's sake.

"Where is it, my lady?"

Margaret's voice intruded on Ellis's thoughts as though from a great distance. "Where is what, Margaret?"

"The babe, my lady," Margaret insisted as she glanced about the room. "You said there was a babe."

"There was." Ellis drew in a shuddering breath. "Jonas had been struggling to find work since his uncle had lost his shop to the banks but, hard as it was, we so looked forward to bringing another life into our lives. Most of the nursery furnishings we had begged or borrowed from what friends we had remaining to us. I was cut off from my family except for the endowment my father left me for my education and that we could not touch. We were both under a lot of strain in those days, but I think that our anticipation of the child kept us together."

Ellis looked again with longing at the empty bassinet.

"It's exactly as I remember it the last time I stood here." Ellis turned slowly in the middle of the room. "I, too, wondered where my child was, Margaret, even though I knew full well I had miscarried."

"Is milady saying that this is a place from your life after you left the Gate?"

"Yes, a terrible, painful place."

"But it's not just a memory, your ladyship," Margaret said in earnest excitement. "I'm here, too. You made this place. You're changing the Day."

"I can't see how," Ellis said, her mind still fixed on the bright pain that the nursery brought to her recollection.

"What else?" Margaret asked in a rush. "What else do you remember?"

"I don't want to remember any more," Ellis insisted.

"Please," Margaret coaxed.

Ellis drew in another deep breath, trying to steady herself before answering. "I remember wondering what to do with the toys Jonas had purchased. We couldn't afford them but Jonas was giddy and unreasonable about . . ."

Ellis stopped, her eyes fixed on the corner of the room behind the door.

She remembered the dollhouse that Jonas had built for their baby and had set in that corner but this one was different from the simple construction she remembered. Though half buried in tin boxes, balls and tops, its silhouette was strikingly familiar.

It was the miniature image of Summersend . . . the cottage in Gamin where she had last seen Jenny.

A box at the base of the dollhouse caught her eye. Like the dollhouse itself, the box was out of place here and not as she remembered the nursery.

She reached down and picked up the box. The label across the front read "Toys made by the Disabled Soldiers & Sailors at the Lord Roberts Memorial Workshops, London, S.W."

As Ellis drew open the top of the box, a strange smile came to her lips.

In the box lay six tin soldiers. Ellis noticed at once that despite the label on the box these tin soldiers were not British at all but were painted with Canadian uniforms and markings. She brought the box closer to her face, trying to see them better in the dim firelight of the room. She suddenly pulled back with a start.

"What is it?" Margaret asked with alarm.

Each of the tin soldiers had been formed as though it was wounded in battle. One had bandages on its face as though it was being treated for mustard gas burns. Others were missing limbs. Some were supported on their bases by crutches.

"I told you I would find soldiers," Ellis said. The giggle in her voice had a hysterical edge. "What better place to look for toy soldiers than in a playroom? But why should anyone want to create such toys?"

"What do you mean, your ladyship?" Margaret asked.

"Well, just look at them!" Ellis insisted, holding the box out toward her maid. "They're horrific toys!"

"What toys, milady?" Margaret asked deliberately.

"These in the box," Ellis insisted, turning the open box back under her gaze. "No child should play with such . . ."

The box in her hand was empty.

"I could not agree with you more on that point, Ellis," said the husky voice behind her.

She looked up from the box.

Six soldiers stood about them in the dark nursery.

Six maimed, horribly disfigured soldiers.

15

SOLDIERS

"Who are you?" Ellis demanded. Her hand that still held the empty box had begun shaking.

"You know us, ma'am." The husky voice belonged to a strong man who was taller than the others. He wore a stained and worn-out field coat with the chevrons of a chief warrant officer. He had a striking, strong jaw and a generous mouth. His brown hair, in some places nearly four inches in length, stuck awkwardly out from beneath the bandage that wrapped around his head, hiding his eyes from view. The man stood very still, as though he were afraid to move from the spot on which he stood. "You know us all."

"Ellis!" Margaret's voice was delighted. "Did you make them?"

"Make them?" Ellis turned her gaze sharply toward her maid.

"Oh, I suppose you didn't; not really," Margaret gushed as she openly gaped at the mutilated men struggling to stand around them. "But aren't they perfectly *horrible*!"

"Margaret!" Ellis felt disgust at her companion's obvious delight in these men's deplorable condition.

"I mean, of course I've seen *Soldiers* before." Margaret could not stop talking. "Not up close, mind you, since Mrs. Crow has forbidden them outside the Ruins. Dr. Carmichael studiously avoided them and Merrick never had much use for them, either. But every time I've seen them, they were always so perfect and whole. These are deliciously broken, like they were in *pieces* or something."

"Margaret, hold your tongue!" Ellis barked in a voice that brooked no disobedience. She had learned that commanding voice from her father and she suddenly recalled that it had gotten her through many difficult encounters with other medical students in her college. She turned back toward the chief. "I beg your pardon for my . . . for my maid, Sergeant Major. She . . . she does not get much out of the house."

A wide grin split the blind sergeant's face. "I do not suppose any of you, how did you put it, 'get much out of the house.' But if you don't act soon, Ellis, we cannot stay."

The door to the closet in the room suddenly burst open. To Ellis's astonishment, beyond was not the small closet she remembered but a white room so brilliant that she could not see into it. Voices were calling in urgent tones from the brightness.

"*Nurse! Get them in here right now! Stop gaping and move!*"

The voice resonated with memory. *That's Dr. Mallory,* she realized. *It was my first day, and he was on duty.*

"*Nurse! For heaven's sake, MOVE!*"

"Margaret," Ellis said at once as she turned toward the sergeant major, and gripped his arm firmly. "Help me get these men through the door. Quickly now!"

"Oh, it really *is* amazing," Margaret gushed.

"Stop talking and help me!" Ellis demanded. "You go through and I'll bring each of them to you through the door!"

Margaret did not have to be told a second time. She stepped quickly through the bright doorway. Ellis brought the sergeant major to the opening first, then each of the others in turn: the dark-haired, swarthy sergeant who had lost his leg, the young man nearly entirely wrapped in bandages, the barrel-chested corporal with the beard and both hands wrapped against his chest, the horribly burned young man with the badly disfigured face, and finally the red-haired, freckled young private with the bleeding ear who only stared into the distance as she gently pushed him ahead of her through the doorway.

Ellis blinked against the bright whiteness around her. Her eyes quickly began to adjust and the features of the room slowly emerged from the brilliant haze.

It was one of the open hospital wards at Massachusetts General. The walls were bright with fresh, white paint. Afternoon light streamed in through the windows. There were six hospital beds in the ward, three on each side, and each gleamed in the afternoon light. Five of the beds were already occupied. Margaret, now somehow dressed in the long gray dress and white bib apron of a nurse with her hair bound tightly beneath a white scarf cap, helped the man with the bleeding ear toward the final berth.

The door behind Ellis clicked quietly shut. She turned toward it, half expecting Dr. Mallory to emerge from the door and begin berating her for not caring for the patients in the manner he prescribed.

"Why are we wasting our time with her?" said the small private to her right. At least, she assumed he was a private given the lack of markings on his jacket that hung next to his bed. His head, chest and arms were completely swathed in bandages though in the areas that were exposed she could clearly see where the blistered skin from the mustard gas had been scraped away. His voice was that of a high tenor but was raspy and rough sounding.

"Don't be that way, Mouse," said the sergeant leaning against the foot rails of the bed across from the private. He was a swarthy man with black hair with naturally tight curls. He had an athletic build. He leaned heavily on a crutch as he was missing his left leg halfway up his calf. Ellis could see that the massive wound was soaking through the bandage.

"And how should I be?" Mouse asked in plaintive tones. "I thought we had agreed to avoid this woman."

"The situation has changed, Private." The blinded master sergeant was feeling his way around the bed.

"How do you figure that, Barry?" This was the barrel-chested man with the rough beard. Both his mangled hands were bandaged and bound against his chest. He lay propped up in his bed, his dark eyes fixed on her as he spoke.

"Because, Tinker, she came looking for us," the master sergeant said. "You must admit, that is rather the opposite of the way we usually operate here, isn't it?"

The man with the bleeding ear giggled at this remark.

"I think she is dangerous." Mouse spoke more forcefully from behind his bandaged mustard blisters. "She has cheated life and death. She is outside the bound of justice."

"But, surely, not outside of mercy." Ellis turned to face the man with the burn-ravaged face and scalp. She fixed on his eyes and discovered them to be a beautiful hazel color.

"Very well, Philly," Master Sergeant Barry called to the bed kitty-corner from his own where the burned man lay. "What do you think?"

"Who are we to measure justice—or mercy," Philly said with slurred speech through his burned lips. "Aren't they both infinite?"

"Neil would know," said the swarthy man with the single leg as he nodded toward the freckle-faced young man with the bleeding ear.

Neil was gazing at the ceiling, holding both his hands out at arm's length with their palms up and rocking from side to side.

"Mouse is right," said the man leaning on his crutch at the foot of his bed. "Power corrupts and absolute power corrupts absolutely. Look at what she's done to us."

"What I've done to *you*?" Ellis said in a voice that demanded their attention.

The Soldiers and Margaret all turned to look at her.

"All I know is that I have to find my way out of this madness and back to my own sanity," Ellis said, her voice lowering into a quiet, restrained quiver. "I need to find my cousin Jenny and the *both* of us need to leave through the Gate. I think I'm beginning to understand how I can find Jenny but I need *you* to show me the way to the Gate."

"And then what, Ellis," said the blind Soldier as he sat on the edge of his bed with his shoulders slumped over. "What happens to you after that? Where do you go? What do you *choose*?"

Ellis opened her mouth to speak but realized she did not know.

"Ellis, don't you remember who we are?" the blind Soldier asked in a whisper.

Ellis glanced down. Her dress was still the terrible, dull green but now she wore a nurse's apron over it. She could feel the cap on her head as she straightened up to look again on the blind Soldier.

"I do remember," she said in soft tones. "This was the ward I served in at Boston Memorial. This is where I first saw soldiers returning from the war."

"That's right." The blind soldier nodded. "What do you remember?"

"I remember . . ." Ellis hesitated, her eyes narrowing. "I remember there were six of you in the ward. I remember treating each of you as calmly as I could manage but inside I was more terrified by the moment."

"Terrified of us?" asked Philly.

"No," Ellis said, shaking her head.

"Terrified for *him*," the blind master sergeant said.

"Yes," Ellis said. The walls of the room felt as though they were closing in on her. It was as though the room were becoming the box . . . the box of broken toy soldiers that she had found in the abandoned nursery.

"For Jonas," Tinker suggested as he cocked his head to one side.

"He was still a Canadian citizen," Ellis said, her eyes blinking back tears. "He was out of work and they drafted him. He had skills as a watchmaker and . . . and he left for the war."

"And so you saw us, here in the box," the blind soldier said and nodded, a tear of his own coursing down his cheek.

"He was so impetuous; so headstrong," Ellis said, the memories of her feelings in the hospital ward rushing over her in waves, threatening to overwhelm her and drag her drowning beneath them. "When his uncle lost the shop to creditors, he struggled to find work but he somehow managed barely from month to month. He so very badly wanted a child and when we lost . . ."

She could not go on.

"When you lost your child." The master sergeant urged her to continue.

Ellis could barely speak the words. "When I . . . mis-carried, we were both of us devastated but somehow it broke Jonas. He grew distant and I thought, perhaps, that he blamed me. I don't think he did, but it poisoned things between us. He stayed out late. Slept late. He seemed to lose interest in any pursuits. When the draft notice came, I wondered if it weren't a relief to both of us to have an excuse to be apart."

"But then you came to the soldiers' ward," said the man with the mustard gas burns.

Ellis nodded, her words soft. "Then I met you."

"But was it really us?" the blind master sergeant asked.

"I . . . what do you mean?" Ellis stammered.

"We are not those men that you met," said Tinker, his hands firmly wrapped against his chest but his grin wide inside the bushy beard. "We look like them because we must—because it is how you relate to us in this place."

Margaret's face was suddenly drained of color. She hurried over toward where Ellis stood and gripped her arm. "We have to go now."

"I . . . I don't understand," Ellis said, shaking off Margaret's grip. "We don't know where the Gate is yet!"

"Do you think this person is actually a nurse?" said Mouse from deep within his bandages as he nodded his head toward Margaret. "She only appears that way because *you* want her to fit into your memory of this place. The world, it seems, is very much what *you* make it."

"Come along, my lady," Margaret hissed. "We have to go now or we'll never find Jenny!"

"Stop it, Margaret!" Ellis snapped. "What do you mean I'm causing all of this? That can't be true. I'm trying to get out of here—not make *more* of it!"

"And, might I add," said the one-legged soldier, "you *really* should have finished your dance with Jonas."

The soldier called Red giggled again, his hands rising into pose for a waltz.

Ellis's jaw dropped.

"They're lying," Margaret said, desperation rising in her voice. "Don't listen to them."

Ellis stepped forward, walking slowly down the row of beds, her eyes fixed on the blind sergeant. Her words were careful and direct. "I asked you before, Sergeant— who are you?"

"You know us, Nurse Harkington, or was it Dr. Kirk?" he said with a wistful smile. "You came into the ward every day after that, sat with us and wrote our letters for us. Each time you left, you stopped at the door and turned to wave to us. We all called out to you. Do you remember what you would call back as you left?"

Ellis nodded.

"I said, 'Good night, my angels!'"

The blind soldier smiled and stood before her. As he did, he grew taller and stronger. His tattered uniform began to gleam like polished metal. A bright aura surrounded his form as he started to rise.

Ellis stepped backward between the beds.

The soldiers on either side, each began to grow and to rise. The deformations of their war wounds melted away and their figures became whole and renewed. Each floated upward into the high ceiling space, their tattered, war-weary uniforms merging into armor so brilliant that Ellis had trouble focusing her eyes on them.

"Ellis! Please!" Margaret shouted. "We can't stay here!"

Great wings unfolded from the backs of the soldiers, their brilliance like the sun.

Ellis could no longer see. Margaret was pulling at her, but she could no longer tell where she was in the hospital ward—if the ward still existed at all.

Her hand brushed against something solid.

Ellis grasped it.

The handle.

She pressed the latch and followed the door as it swung open, tumbling to the floor with Margaret falling next to her. She heard more than saw the door close behind them.

The painful brilliance faded from her eyes and she struggled to her knees and looked up.

She was completely unprepared for what she saw.

She was kneeling on the inlaid parquet floor in the entry of Summersend.

16

THE PLACE

Ellis stood still in the middle of the parquet floor. She stared at the broken and faded patterns of it beneath her feet. It was entirely familiar and terrible all at once. This place belonged in Gamin . . . or somewhere . . . anywhere but here in this madness of Echo House.

The main rotunda extended overhead to the upper floors, accessed by the familiar curved staircase, but the wallpaper had mostly curled away from the curving wall except in a few of the corner spaces. The plaster on the walls was stained and had fallen away from the lathe work in several locations. The balusters of the once elegantly curved handrail were broken outward near the bottom of the stairs, causing the upper handrail to hang precariously toward the modest, web-covered chandelier overhead. Ellis was afraid to move for fear the entire crystal assembly would come loose from the ceiling and crash down on them both.

Opposite the clock and broken bench, the small side table leaned precariously against the wall. Atop it sat the bell jar, now nearly entirely obscured with dust above its weathered, wooden base. Ellis fixed her eyes on it, trying to peer through the dirty glass without success.

"It's Summersend!" cried Margaret in genuine delight. "However did you manage it?"

Ellis turned slowly around. Behind them was the short hallway to the salon, the bookcase alcove to one side. On her right were the remains of the narrow bench, its legs broken on one end. The grandfather clock standing next to it was covered in a moldering sheet. Ellis had a sudden dread of lifting it up and seeing what remained beneath it. Before her was the entry hall with double doors on either side. The doors to the left had fallen from their hinges and sat askew in the archway. She could barely make out the dark shapes of the shuttered music room just beyond. At the end of the hall was the door through which they had just come; the front door of Summersend. Its paint had peeled away and cracks had appeared in the weathered wood but brilliant light was still streaming through its cracked frosted panes.

"Tell me how you did it," Margaret demanded breathlessly. "So perfect; so quickly!"

"I . . . I don't know," Ellis said, gazing about her in stunned reverence. Her eyes returned to the side table against the wall near her left hand and opposite the bench. The enormous bell jar with the darkly stained and lacquered base was still sitting on its surface, but now it was almost completely filled with dead lunar moths. "I didn't do anything!"

"But you said you created the house," Margaret urged, the hint of desperation in her voice. "That you were *still* creating it! You wondered if this were *still* your Day!"

"But I haven't *done* anything," Ellis pleaded.

"Liar!" Margaret rushed toward her, gripping Ellis by the shoulders as she gazed purposefully into her eyes. "It isn't your Day, it's Merrick's Day, yet somehow you managed to change circumstances to suit you. Where does this come from, Ellis? How do you make it real?"

"Margaret, stop!" Ellis cried out, struggling to get loose from the woman's powerful grip. "I don't know how it happens!"

Ellis broke free of Margaret, rushing toward the front door.

"Ellis, no!" Margaret warned, her voice harsh and menacing. "Don't make me stop you!"

The light streaming through the frosted glass became dimmer with each step Ellis took. It had nearly vanished entirely as she grasped the door handle, turned it and pulled the door wide.

Ellis reeled back from the precipice at the doorstep.

The space beyond had changed.

She teetered on the brink of an elevator shaft. The rough, brick walls both descended into the depths and ascended into the heights beyond the limits of her vision. Doorways, patterned identically to the one in which she stood, exited the shaft at each level below her. Rusting guide rails on both sides and a set of cables running down the center of the shaft gave mind-spinning perspective to the depths beckoning her to fall into its maw.

Ellis drew back into the hall in a panic, slamming the door shut with a violent shove. She backed slowly past twisted doors to the music room until she bumped against the grandfather clock. Its chimes rattled discordantly behind her.

"So that is it." Margaret smiled back at Ellis from the rotunda at the opposite end of the entry hall. The lady's maid took several hesitant steps toward Ellis across the floor. "That's how you do it!"

"Margaret," Ellis said with quiet caution. "How I do what?"

"All this." Margaret gestured toward the expanse of the house about them. "The house, the sky, the Day . . . I understand how you do it now . . . I understand *everything.*"

Ellis stood with her back against the clock, her eyes fixed on her lady's maid. "What do you understand, Margaret?"

"The Day does not come from your *thoughts,* it comes from somewhere deeper within," Margaret said with savory relish. "It's not a rational choice of will. It comes from *desire* . . . it comes from the place of *dreams*!"

"Margaret, I don't understand."

"Yes, yes, you do!" Margaret insisted, her bright eyes burning with fanatical passion. "Think, Ellis! Out of all the possible creations you might make real in your Day . . . out of an infinity of possible places to fall into . . . why *this* place? Why Summersend?"

Ellis thought.

She drew in a breath.

"Why Summersend indeed?" came another, deeper voice from the direction of the broken doors of the music room.

Merrick moved slowly from the shadows, stepping carefully between the broken doors of the hall. He was in full morning dress with a coat and waistcoat that were perfectly tailored for him. The high, turndown collar capped his striped shirt and framed the knot of his silk tie in exact symmetry. The striped trousers had creases as straight and sharp as a knife.

Merrick stopped and stood just outside of the music room, cocking his head to one side as he considered the two women in the rotunda. He drew his long, delicate hands upward at his sides in a deliberate motion, flicking back the edges of his coat and slipping both into the pockets of his trousers.

"You've led us all a merry chase, Ellis," Merrick said,

his eyes watery and large. "I had hoped you would have at least stayed until the end of the play."

"I didn't think I would care for the ending." Ellis shivered slightly.

"Well, let's just say it's a work in progress." Merrick shrugged, a painful smile flitting across his lips. "But Margaret asked a most excellent question, my dear Lady Ellis: why Summersend? It was never our house in our Day, and yet here it stands around us in the Ruins, sad and forgotten."

"It was in Gamin, too," Ellis said as much to herself as to Merrick. "Why was it there?"

"It was for you." Merrick took a step forward, his hands slipping from his pockets, reaching forward as though there were a present in his hands. "It was all for you. The town, the people, the mansion and even this—even Summersend—because you loved it so and I wanted to be the one who gave it back to you. Me. From me. I wanted to give it to you. It should have been from *me*!"

Merrick strode toward Ellis suddenly. Ellis pushed away from the clock but it was too late. Merrick's hands reached up, gripping her face on either side so firmly that her vision blurred. He pulled her back in front of him, his terrible dark eyes burning inches from her own.

"But it wasn't the house at all, was it?" Merrick's lips quivered now as he spoke, his eyes fixed with a fevered stare. "It wasn't the house or the dresses or the town or the sea or the sky! It was *him,* wasn't it? He sat by the Gate and waited for you like some lovesick puppy who just wouldn't go home. And when you came to the Gate, what did he do, Ellis? What did he *do*?"

"I don't know!" Ellis cried out through her sobs. "I don't remember!"

"I remember! I remember it all!" Merrick shouted into her face. "I remember him tearing you apart! I remember that he waited and waited and then when you came to the Gate he saw his chance and stole you away from everything we had built and loved. I remember that he would rather *cripple* you than let you be great with me!"

"Merrick, don't!" Margaret pleaded as she tried to pull his grip loose from Ellis's face.

Merrick shifted his grip, clasping Ellis's narrow jaw in his left hand as he snatched at Margaret's arm. In a moment, he twisted the arm of the lady's maid painfully around the woman's back. Her feet were barely touching the floor when he threw her with all his force into the short hall behind her. Margaret crashed against the bookcase, the weathered tomes disintegrating with the impact as she slumped sobbing to the floor.

Merrick twisted Ellis around in his iron, unyielding grip, pushing her head against the curved wall opposite the stairs. She could feel the weight of his body pressing against hers, pinning her.

Again he gripped her on both sides of her face, holding her so that she was forced to look into his face. His lips were parted in agony, tears streaming from his eyes, but she could see no humanity, no compassion within them—only an unending void.

"I loved you so, Ellis." Merrick shook as he spoke. "You came for me—you chose *me*! We left the war behind us, you and I. The others, they made their choice and the war went on without us. They sent us here, thinking it was a punishment but it wasn't that at all. They said that we were damned—damned to be who we were and nothing more. But who we were was mighty, Ellis. Serve in heaven or serve in hell—there is no choice in that—but *here* we were . . . I made you the mistress of all the Tween. I was the one who gave you everything! I was the one who made a place where we could be!"

Ellis could barely move against the weight of him pressing her into the wall. He had raised her up, her feet no longer touching the floor and flailing about beneath her. Ellis cast her eyes frantically about her, searching for something . . . anything.

Her eyes fell on the large bell jar on the table next to them.

"Merrick! Please!" she begged.

The man's lips curled back into a horrible smile, pain filling his eyes a hand's breadth from her face. "Please? Isn't that all I've ever tried to do? But you're not pleasing me back, Ellis! *You* made this house for us. It was the very first house of our existence and you made this Day for *me*! For *ME*!"

Merrick lifted her up higher onto the wall. Ellis was finding it hard to breathe. Her eyes fixed on the bell jar on the table.

Moths. It was filled with moths.

One of their wings fluttered.

"And now I find *this* abomination in the Ruins?" Merrick seethed. "It wasn't the house at all, was it, Ellis? It was for *him*! It was because of *him*!"

Ellis kicked sideways with her left foot. It did not connect with the table as firmly as she had hoped but the decayed condition of the wood yielded at once to the blow. The far leg snapped and the table shifted as it fell, sliding the bell jar across its surface.

The bell jar crashed against the parquet floor, shattering at once.

Moths—a thousand and more—erupted from the confines of the glass. They filled the rotunda of the house in a thick whirlwind of gray and color, their wings beating against the faces of everyone in the room as they passed in their frantic flight.

Merrick cried out, releasing his grip on Ellis's face in favor of shielding his own. Ellis dropped down the wall and fell to the floor on her side. The moths flew above her, whirling about Merrick, their delicate wings rushing in to brush against his face before they again entered the cloud of moths whirling about the rotunda.

Merrick reeled back from them, crying out in angry frustration. For a moment he stood swatting in panic at the moths darting about his face, then he turned and ran toward the front of the hall.

The door flew open before Merrick as he approached, still revealing the elevator shaft that had so startled Ellis long moments before. Merrick lunged out the door, howling as he dove into the shaft, the door slamming shut behind him against the onslaught of moths.

Ellis slumped to the floor, leaning against the rough surface of the rotunda wall. She felt exhausted—spent—and barely able to lift her eyes to gaze expectantly down the foyer hall.

Memories drew up unbidden within her.

She knew what was coming.

The moths wheeled at the door, a cyclone of gray and color spinning around an axis. The whirling mass at once both contracted and became more complex, the dance of the moths in the air fragmenting into appendages to the core mass. The frantically beating figures were resolving into a tighter form with arms, legs and a head. One of the larger moths flitted at the face, its broad wings forming a mask where the patterns appeared as blank, turquoise eyes.

Margaret let out a short, piercing scream.

It was the figure of a man composed entirely of moths. Their wings still fluttered across the surface of its skin. A second large moth took its place on the face, its wings forming a paisley blotch on the right side of the moth-man's face.

Ellis sat up slightly, bracing her back against the curve

of the wall behind her. Merrick's question still raged in her mind. *It wasn't this house at all, was it? It was for* him, *wasn't it?*

The figure took a step toward the women.

The paint on the door melted back into place, brightening to a shine as the weathered surface flattened back as though new. The dust vanished from the frosted glass and morning light beyond streamed through it, casting the moth-man in silhouette.

"Why this place?" Ellis murmured. "Why Summersend?"

Ellis thought for a moment. Both here and in Gamin, this home was important to her. Something had happened here, something she wanted desperately to remember.

The moths' wings began to merge tighter still as the changes to the door began to spread to the hallway around it.

And continued to spread toward Margaret and Ellis.

17

SUMMER'S END

Stop him!" Margaret insisted.

"I don't think I can," Ellis sighed.

The moth-man took another step toward them, swaying slightly in the hall. With each passing moment, the moths were grouping tighter together, their colors merging into a uniform smoothness of cloth, thread and skin. The coat was different now, a long military tunic emerging with two breast pockets beneath an open trench coat. The writhing moths at the figure's head stiffened into a peaked hat, its visor suddenly shining in the hall light.

"But you stopped Merrick!" There was panic in Margaret's voice. "No one has ever managed to do that . . . ever!"

"But I wanted to stop Merrick. I don't think I want

to stop this one." Ellis pulled her feet painfully under her, pushing against the floor as she slid her back up the wall.

"After all he's done to you?" Margaret's voice broke as she spoke. "He stole you away from us . . . from your home."

"I think I want him to come," Ellis said. "That's why he's here at all. I think I need to face him."

It was as though a wave of the past were washing down the hall from around the shadowed figure before them. The paint along the chair rail curled back into place, brightening to a shine. The broken railing of the curving staircase groaned back into place as the broken balusters mended one by one. The plaster gathered from the floor and the winds, choking the hallway with dust for a moment before filling in the holes in the walls and covering the lathe beneath with perfect smoothness.

"Ellis?" Margaret's voice quivered.

Tears filled Ellis's eyes. She could not move. Dared not breathe.

She *remembered*.

Jonas stood before her, gazing at her with a thousand hopes, apologies and questions.

He was as she remembered him on that day. His face was marred from the horrible burn that ran as a paisley-shaped mark over his right eye. His infantryman uniform was a bit rumpled from the journey but his tie was straight and he had done what he could to look presentable despite the hurried journey down from Halifax. His eyes were bright and liquid as he removed his peaked hat.

They stood facing each other in the hall of Summersend as they had once before—so very far away and so long ago.

Ellis lifted her chin and drew in a deep breath. "You were the one who waited for me by the Gate."

"Yes." Jonas nodded with a shy smile. "Yes, I waited."

"I never gave you any cause for hope . . . never encouraged your attentions," Ellis said, her mouth feeling dry. "Yet you waited for me all the same."

Jonas nodded.

"Why, Jonas?" she asked. "Why?"

Jonas looked up, his loving gaze moving about the hallway. He did not answer her at once. He drew in a deep, satisfied breath before his eyes fell on her again.

"You baked bread," he said.

Ellis's eyes narrowed. What he had said was some complete non sequitur and yet somehow his words resonated in her mind. "I don't . . . what do you mean?"

"Remember, Ellis," Jonas said. "I came in the front door. It was in the afternoon with the sunlight streaming in through the glass of the front door, just as it is now. I think I must have stood on that porch for almost half an hour trying to decide whether to ring the doorbell or just come in. I finally realized how ridiculous it looked for a soldier to be standing on the porch without the courage to enter your uncle's summer home. So, at last, I turned the doorknob and stepped into the hall. That's when I saw you, coming from the kitchen into the rotunda."

Ellis smelled the warm, inviting aroma of baking loaves filling the air from the back of the house. She pushed herself away from the wall and stood, uncertainly, to face him.

"We looked at each other for what seemed forever," Jonas continued, a tincture of desperation coloring his words. "I was so afraid that you would find me hideous from my wound despite what you had written. Neither of us speaking. Finally, I said . . ."

"You said that I had baked bread," Ellis murmured. "Then I said . . . I said . . ."

"Go on, Ellis." Jonas nodded. "Then you said . . ."

Ellis looked up. The hall around her was restored, clean and bright as it had been in that place and time so far away.

"For you," Ellis echoed her own words from the past.

"I am so sorry, El," he stammered.

"Yes, that is what you said next." Ellis stood very still, as though moving might break the fragile moment. "And do you remember my answer?"

Jonas swallowed, glancing down at the floor before he continued.

Ellis smiled slightly to herself. "I believe my line was, 'Yes, you are a sorry sight indeed.'"

Jonas's face brightened, his spirit rising like the dawn after a long night.

"It was my uncle's house," Ellis said softly, her eyes taking in the hall and staircase as though she were seeing them with new eyes. "We had very little money of our own after the wedding but my uncle owned this summer home . . ."

"In Maine," Jonas prompted.

"Yes, in Maine." Ellis nodded. "We came all the way up on the train so that we could spend our wedding night here."

"It was the happiest day of my life, Ellis." Jonas smiled.

"Perhaps it was," Ellis sighed. "But this isn't that day, is it, Jonas?"

Jonas paused, taking a step back.

"No, Ellis." Jonas's smile fell slightly. "It's a more important day. A stronger day. A more difficult day. A better day."

"This day was years later. You had been gone a long time, Jonas," Ellis said, more accusation in her voice than she intended.

Pain registered at the corner of the young soldier's eyes. "Your constable friends were pretty clear about staying away after they threw me out of our apartments."

"You were impossible to live with." Ellis shook her head, setting her jaw at the memory. "You had such a temper and were so jealous all the time."

"I couldn't believe that you really wanted me, even then," Jonas said through a bitter smile. "You were so beautiful, so bright . . . you seemed so far above me.

When it looked as though we were going to have a child, I thought this would make it all right; this would be the one thing that would bind you to me . . . the one thing that would insure that you would stay with me and never leave."

Ellis took a step toward him, folding her arms across her chest, her words filled with anger and pain.

"But I lost that child, Jonas!"

The shock of the realization suddenly overwhelmed her. Her words were suddenly choked off in a sob. She reached up, furiously brushing at the tears that welled out of her eyes before folding her arms before her again.

"Yes, Ellis." Jonas nodded. "*We* lost that child."

"Our child died within me," Ellis said, her lips quivering with anger and regret.

"It wasn't just our child that died that day."

"No," Ellis spoke between stifling sobs. "So much more than our child."

"It's all right," Jonas said, reaching his arms out for her. He folded her in his own arms, cradling her there as best he could despite her arms remaining crossed against him.

"You blamed me," Ellis sniffed.

"I blamed myself," Jonas said quietly against her cheek.

"What difference did it make in the end," Ellis said. She lifted her hands up against his chest, pushing away slightly from his embrace. "It *felt* as though I were to blame. Every time you looked at me . . . every time you touched me, you took it out on me."

"I took it out on us both," Jonas said. "I was in such pain, Ellis. I just didn't know how to tell you. By the time I determined to make it right, I'd been drafted. The army needed skilled craftsmen for the engineer corps and I was still a Canadian citizen. By then it was too late to turn back and I was overseas. I wrote to you every day, hoping that you might one day be moved by my letters to write me back. Then after I got my medical discharge and you did write me at last . . ."

"I asked you to meet me here," Ellis said.

"Yes, here." Jonas nodded. "The one place where we could come where we could set aside what had happened and try to start over despite our wounds. And we did start over, Ellis. Here, in those glorious few days we spent together, we were able to forget . . ."

"Forget?" Ellis said sharply. She pushed away from him with her arms as she stepped back. "All I've done is forget. Long before I met you in that clock shop, I'd forgotten an entire existence here before I was born. Forgotten that it was you who lured me through the Gate out of this place. It was the sight of you on the other side that drew me on, curious as to how you could possibly be there. Then what did you do, Jonas? Kidnap me into mortality?"

"No, Ellis, I couldn't possibly . . ."

"I just *fell* into the world by accident, I suppose!"

"No, Ellis! Of course not!" Jonas protested. "I had won the confidence of one of the Guardians . . ."

"But as I understand it, it was you who arranged to lure

me out of the Tween and send me into the world," Ellis said, her anger rising by the moment. "Whether you did it yourself or convinced someone else to help you, you dragged me away from this place and pushed me into a mortal life!"

"That's right, my lady," Margaret said as she stepped up behind her. "And being mortal, you would have forgotten everything that happened before. Your home here, Merrick, Alicia, Silenus, Ely, me . . . everyone that you knew and everything that you ever made here was swept from your memory. All you knew was mortal, and Jonas counted on that!"

"Was that it?" Ellis looked Jonas in the eye, fixing her gaze on him. "You thought that if you somehow managed to drag me into mortality that you would have a better chance at somehow winning my heart?"

"Well, yes . . . no . . . It's not that simple!"

"No, it's not simple at all and it seems to me to be even a great deal *more* complicated than you think!" Ellis's voice grew firm and accusing. "If I understand what is supposed to have happened here, you somehow arranged for both of us to be born about the same time. But it doesn't seem like a particularly elegant plan since I was born in Boston and you were born somewhere in the eastern provinces of Canada! Just how did you expect our paths to cross when we couldn't remember anything about each other?"

"Well, that part *is* a bit complicated," Jonas stammered.

"Indeed?" Ellis seethed. "And the explanation is . . . what?"

"We have no memories of our lives here but who we were here resonates as a thread of who we are in the next life," Jonas said, gnawing at his lip as he tried to explain. "I knew that our lives here would converge there and that I at last could take care of you as I always hoped I could. It's not destiny, exactly, so much as a convergence like a river of our choices, which—"

"I don't want to hear it!" Ellis yelled. She turned from him, pacing back and forth in the hall before him. "I'm tired of being 'cared for' or 'manipulated' or 'saved' . . . I don't *need* to be saved, Jonas! I never *did*. I didn't need someone to take care of me, guide me or protect me. I needed someone I could stand beside, who wasn't afraid of the woman I could become and who would encourage me to be stronger, not weaker."

"Then why come back here?" Jonas shot back, his own anger rising. "If you have been so determined to be strong, why return to this prison of the twice damned!"

"I came back for Jenny!" Ellis shouted. She stopped in her tracks, facing Jonas squarely. "I didn't know it then, but I know it now. I have to find her and then we have to leave the Gate together. And you're going to show us the way."

"But I don't know where Jenny is," Jonas protested.

"Well, what do you know?" Ellis demanded.

"Those who come from the outside—from beyond the

Tween—have a sense of where others like us can be found," Jonas admitted. "It's how we find the Gates and each other here in the Tween. I think I may be able to find the Gate but not even the Soldiers know where she is hiding. I've already asked them."

"My lady?"

Ellis turned in surprise toward the quiet voice that called down to her from the stairs. "Alicia! How did you get here?"

"I was with Jonas," she said, calling down from the landing above. She started down the stairs as she spoke, still wearing her now somewhat tattered Egyptian-themed costume from the masquerade. "I was checking the upstairs for Jenny when I overheard your conversation."

"What of it, Alicia?" Margaret asked, deep suspicion obvious in her tone.

Alicia stepped from the stairs onto the rotunda floor, facing Ellis.

"Well, it occurs to me, your ladyship," Alicia said with a coy lift of her eyebrows, "that if a Soldier doesn't know where Jenny is, then perhaps their opposite number might?"

"You mean, if one of my angels won't do . . ."

"Then what we need is a devil." Alicia nodded.

Merrick plunged down the endless elevator shaft headfirst, the tails of his morning coat flapping at his back. He

snarled at the air as it rushed past. His held out his hands
and arms, bringing him to face the bottomless abyss.

He bent his mind to the problem . . . and bent the shaft
in turn.

Slowly, his surroundings shifted. The doors to the rap-
idly passing floors remained oriented to the vertical but
the shaft rotated slightly from vertical and became an
acutely angled passage. His feet connected gently against
the slope that had been the back wall of the elevator shaft.
Though his speed was still great, it was enough to begin
slowing his momentum.

The chute continued to turn while the doors rotated
in place. Soon the chute became a ramp and then fully
horizontal to become a hall down which Merrick was
sliding across the wooden floor that formed beneath him.

His foot caught on a tattered rug.

Merrick tumbled down the hall, rolling for nearly
twenty feet before at last coming to a stop. He picked
himself up slowly, brushing the dust from the old ruin of
a hall from his morning coat.

He knew from the condition of the hall he had just
transformed that he was still in the Ruins of Echo House.
He also knew that things were not going according to
his will in a place where his will was everything.

He considered the hallway. There was no reason why
he should be constrained by the inconvenience of logic,
space or time. The hall appeared to go forever in either
direction and, he supposed, he could go back the way he

had fallen and come to where he had been surprised by Jonas. He might more confidently find Ellis there but he abhorred the idea of succumbing to such mundane constraints as walking.

He always preferred to write the rules rather than obey them.

His smiled as the thought suddenly vanished. There was a change in the air, a chill that he could feel approaching. The transformed shaft was well lit for a hallway but now the distant ends of it were darkened and growing dim and dull in his vision.

Shades, he thought. *The Shades approach and that can only mean . . .*

The door in front of him opened.

"Mrs. Crow," Merrick muttered.

"My lord," the old woman acknowledged.

The Shades were drawing close to him from both ends of the hall. He could not see but a few feet beyond them as they approached. Merrick could pick out their forms in the hallway, what had been, or could have been, men and women shifting in their forms as they approached. Merrick could see his breath exhaled as wispy clouds into the frigid air before him.

He turned to face Mrs. Crow. "A rather nice touch, Mrs. Crow, considering I have never drawn breath."

"We must keep up appearances, my lord," Mrs. Crow said with a nod of her pleasant face and a thin smile. "Is Lady Ellis any closer to finding her prize?"

"How should I know," Merrick snarled. "I don't know where she is hidden, either."

"But they are close to finding someone who does," Mrs. Crow said agreeably. "And when they do, we shall all have our reward."

18

FIGUREHEAD

Where are you going now, Ellis?" Jonas called to her, but she was already pushing past Margaret through the short hall at the back of the rotunda.

"Into the trap," Ellis responded over her shoulder as she rushed down the entryway. She swung abruptly through the open doors on the left and into the music room, the same room from which Merrick had emerged just minutes before. It had been a ruin at that time but now was restored to pristine beauty. The piano sat in its familiar place, its case polished and shining in the light streaming through the window. It occurred to Ellis that the garden should be outside those windows and the bay beyond but even as the idea rose to conscious thought she knew that if she parted the lace and curtains she would only be looking into another compartment of Echo House. The loss and disappointment of that idea only steeled her resolve.

She turned again and stepped up to the little built-in bookcase. There, as she expected, was a small vase.

"Ellis, wait," Alicia pleaded as she trailed Jonas and Margaret into the room. "Perhaps we need to discuss this among ourselves and come up with a better plan than walking into a trap."

The vase before Ellis was filled with dead flowers.

She smiled. "Except that it is *my* trap."

Ellis reached up, lifting the vase off of its shelf. As it had before, she heard with satisfaction the click of the lock release.

"I'm not sure this is a good idea, Ellis," Jonas said, the color draining from his face.

"I trapped you in here once before," Ellis acknowledged as she pulled open the hidden doorway. "This time, we'll all keep you company."

The doorway swung open, illuminated from the room beyond with a dull red, flickering light. Ellis took a deep breath to steady her own resolve as she leaned inside the secret doorway for a look beyond.

The walls and ceiling of the room beyond were configured as she remembered them, a small, hidden craft room that she had specifically designed as a trap back in the world of Gamin. To Ellis, this meant that this incarnation of the house was not the one she remembered from the real world of mortality but the strange, dreamlike world of the Tween.

The striking difference was the complete absence of a floor. Instead of the polished hardwoods she remembered, a wide staircase descended at a precipitous angle down toward depths illuminated by red-tinted hurricane lamps. The chair rail paneling on the wall extended downward to meet the frighteningly steep stairs where they entered a cellar.

"What's down there?" Margaret gave Ellis a questioning glance as she spoke.

"I . . . I think . . . is that hell?" Alicia whimpered.

"No, I think it just looks like hell," Ellis said, nodding as much to herself as to her companions. "We're actually way past hell, if the Disir sisters are to be believed. You said we needed to ask a devil, Alicia. I believe this is the best place for us to look to find one."

"And how did you know it was here?" Margaret asked.

"Because I needed it," Ellis said as she stepped onto the staircase. The tread groaned under her weight. "There are rules to this place, Margaret. I'm learning the rules."

"My lady?" Margaret was at her heels. "Where are you going?"

"Where I must," Ellis answered. She did not hesitate. For the first time in a long time there was a surety to her steps. She moved at once, each tread groaning beneath her. The stairs turned and continued downward between the red-glass hurricane lamps. Instead of growing cooler, the air became drier and hotter with every step.

Ellis hurried down the abrupt descent with purpose, the tumble of her footsteps mixed with the voices that fell in her wake.

"Ellis, no," Jonas pleaded.

"Wait for us!" Alicia called out.

Ellis paid them little heed. *Jonas who sat by the Gate. Alicia and Margaret who dreamed of their own Day.* They would follow her, she realized, as they had always followed her.

The staircase emerged high on a cliff wall of an underground cavern. Ellis drew in a deep breath. The near walls were illuminated by the red lanterns but she could not make out their extents on either side. Nor could she see the bottom of the chasm beneath her. Only the continuing descent of the stairs before her.

"I don't remember your uncle's cellar being quite this big," Jonas quipped.

"I don't remember you ever going down there," Ellis said with a smirk.

"It was dark," Jonas said in his defense.

"Not this dark," Ellis said, gathering her courage. "This is the way. Come on."

"I thought I was supposed to guide you?" Jonas said.

Ellis thought for a moment then turned to Jonas. The paisley-shaped bruise over his right eye had become the disfigurement of a burn. Ellis could see the scarring of the tissue, the pulling of facial cartilage. There were a lot of the soldiers who were returning with injuries far worse. She had treated so many of them after she had entered into the nursing corps, the only branch of the service available to her. She was overtrained and overqualified but after Jonas had been drafted into the Canadian services, she had somehow woken up from the pain and the loss to realize that she had thrown away a great deal more. Somehow it felt that if she could serve the warriors coming home she might somehow be serving him, too. There was a penitence that she found comforting and somehow basically right. Her uniform was an outward symbol of that inner regret. It was certainly far less fashionable than she was used to and the color was . . .

Ellis glanced down at the hideous traveling dress she wore.

It was not a traveling dress at all. Though it was devoid of any of the chevrons, badges or patches it was that dull green color and unquestionably the remains of her uniform.

Ellis turned back to face Jonas on the stairs.

"Jonas." Her voice was soft and spoke his name with a tenderness that surprised her. "I don't think I want you to lead me anywhere anymore . . . and I don't want you to follow me, either . . ."

She could see the pain fill his eyes, so she rushed her words, gently placing her hand on his chest. "But what I want . . . what I think I've always wanted . . . was someone who would stand beside me. I know you loved me,

Jonas, and have always wanted what you honestly believed was best for me. And the more I remember of our life together, the more I believe that I had come to love you, too. But I don't need you to save me, Jonas. I know that you will always place my needs ahead of your own. But what I truly wish to know is that you'll place the two of us together ahead of either of us."

She reached down and took his hand.

"Can we face this together?" she asked.

"Together, Ellis," Jonas said, intertwining his fingers with hers.

"That was a lovely scene and I'm sure both Margaret and I are grateful to have been a part of it," Alicia said from behind them. She was shivering visibly. "But now that you know where you keep this demon of yours, could we possibly go back up the stairs now?"

"No," Ellis answered with a firmer determination than she had known since she awoke in this place. "Never go back, Alicia. What's done is done and cannot be undone. Never forget where you've been, but never, ever go back."

"I don't understand," Alicia whined.

"Exactly," Ellis responded. She started down the staircase, with Jonas by her side. There was no railing on the left of the stairs and the railing on the right shifted loosely under her grip. However, to her relief, there were just enough lanterns hanging at uneven intervals down the railing. They could make out further lamps down before them, each barely sufficient for them to see their next few steps ahead. The air grew warmer with every step and uncomfortably damp. The stairs seemed to descend interminably.

"Did you make this?" Margaret asked.

"I honestly don't know, Margaret," Ellis replied.

The descent seemed interminable with the moments stretching into hours. At last, however, something could dimly be perceived emerging from the gloom below. A dark, enormous shape lit by the same dull, red lanterns that had illuminated the upper staircase.

Ellis called softly back, "I think we've found it—or it has found us."

"What do you mean?" Alicia shivered.

"I'm not sure," Ellis answered back in hushed tones.

The shape as a whole was that of an enormous building, an inverted cathedral whose spires were driven into the rock at its base. The uttermost extents could not be determined as they faded into the darkness beyond the extents of their vision both beyond and overhead. It might have been an extension of Echo House thrust downward from the cavernous ceiling above but the closer they got, the more it was evident that the entire monstrous structure was an amalgamation from parts of a chaotic and eclectic assortment of ships. It looked as though the hands of a titan's child had pushed together schooners, barques, steamers and ketches into a broken mass and tried to shape them into a Gothic stalactite. Bowed hulls stood on end, strangely angled turrets standing on a stone island rising from the bottomless chasm below. Masts and rigging stuck out at odd angles from the central mass.

Ellis and Jonas stepped off the bottom of the stairs with Alicia and Margaret close at their heels. The twisted masts, rigging, deck planking and ribbing were illuminated in various places with the same red hurricane lanterns that had lit their way on the way down the long stairs. It cast a dim light that still left the full extents of the structure obscured in the distance.

"There doesn't appear to be a door," Margaret suggested.

"Then, perhaps, we need to find another way in." Ellis released Jonas's hand and walked quickly toward the jumble of the building. She began examining the exterior in its detail. One fantail, upside down to her point of view, read *Monte Blanche*. A vertical bow nearby displayed the name *Imo*. There was even a piece of plating with the name *Titanic* and a wooden stern labeled *Hesperus*.

"What are we looking for?" Margaret asked.

Though her hull was weathered, Ellis could still barely make out the faded name on the side just aft of the bow.

"The *Mary Celeste*," Ellis murmured to herself with satisfaction. Then she raised her hands, cupping around her mouth as she called out, "Ahoy the boat!"

"Ellis," Jonas asked, urgency in his voice, "where are you taking us?"

"Have you ever heard the phrase 'the devil to pay'?" Ellis asked him in return.

"Yes, of course," Jonas answered, still perplexed.

"But do you know the origin of the term?" Ellis grinned.

"What does that have to do with anything?" Alicia blinked, trying to follow the conversation.

"'The devil to pay' is an old sailing phrase," Ellis said. "My father was a doctor but he loved sailing. He never went to sea, but he loved visiting the Boston docks and telling me everything he had read about or learned from the sailors who he treated from the ships. He told me that the 'devil' was the seams between the planks of the old sailing ships. To 'pay' a seam was to caulk it with tar and hemp rope."

"Fascinating," Alicia said flatly as she shrugged. "So?"

"You said we needed to find a devil and that's what we're doing," she responded, then called out loudly again. "Ahoy, Captain!"

"Go away . . ."

Ellis jumped slightly at the sound. It was a creaking voice that had spoken to her and just a few feet above her head.

"Go away!"

Ellis looked up.

Above her was the bow of the *Mary Celeste.* The bowsprit was gone, but there was now a large figurehead whose shape emerged from the wood of the keel. It began at the torso and was, remarkably, the bare-chested figure of a man. The arms swept backward from the shoulders, ending just above the elbow where the arms merged with the hull. The head, however, hung down and gazed with despair back toward the keel. It was a hideous figurehead for a ship: a tortured seaman trapped as part of the ship on which he served.

Even with its head bowed down and turned away from her, Ellis recognized the figurehead.

"Manners, Captain," called Ellis upward softly.

"Ain't interested in manners," the carved statue called back.

"A trade, then, Captain Walker?" Ellis said in gentle response. "Surely you wouldn't pass up a trade?"

The gaunt form raised his head. He had a hound-dog face though its features appeared to be made of weathered wood, cracked like long vertical scars up the face. There was an eternal sadness about his dull eyes as he looked back at them.

"Ye have nothing that I'd care for," the captain called back. "Away with ye."

"I have one thing," Ellis replied.

"And that be?"

She turned and gestured toward Jonas.

"I have a soldier," Ellis said. "And he can find the Gate."

The figurehead Captain Walker shook and as he did the length of the hull groaned and creaked ominously behind him. "What good is that to me now?"

"Because I can free you," Ellis said, then swallowed. *I hope that I can free you.*

"You know who holds me here?" Isaiah quieted down as he spoke.

"Yes," Ellis said clearly. "And I need to see him."

"You won't be back," Isaiah said, shaking his creaking head, drops of tar falling from his eyes in his pain. "He won't let you."

"We will be back for you, Isaiah," Ellis said to the wooden figurehead above her. "Of anyone you know in the Tween, you know that I will come back for you."

"You left *her* behind," Isaiah said with a mixture of hope and accusation.

"Yes, I left her behind." Ellis nodded. "And I came back for her, didn't I?"

The figure at the prow of the *Mary Celeste* nodded with a slight smile. He pulled back his head, his mouth opening into a terrible, silent scream. As he did so, the hull planks began to bend. On either side of the bow, they separated with a popping noise from the keel, pulling back and exposing the ribs of the hull behind them. Then the ribs themselves separated from the keel, as though a chest cavity were being pulled open to expose the lungs and heart beneath.

Ellis took a step back.

Warm, golden light spilled out from behind the spreading of the shattered hull. Ellis could see a twisting hall beyond lit with unsteady, electric bulbs. It appeared to be a wrenched ship's corridor that wound into the bowels of the broken, derelict ships.

"You know he is waiting for you," the figurehead said.

"I know," Ellis said as she stepped over the broken bow of the *Mary Celeste* and into the twisting corridor lit with the flickering, yellow light beyond.

19

LIBRARY

Ellis stepped cautiously down the hallway. It reminded her strongly of a luxurious ship she had visited with her father as a child in Boston Harbor, only now the gleaming white paint was splintered and the bright brass fittings twisted with the torquing of the hallway frames. There was a handrail of polished oak that ran bent and warped between the fittings, which she followed down the hall. Broken doors to staterooms on either side stood ajar and beckoned her with bright colors and even the soft strains of phonograph music could be heard from a few. Ellis ignored the temptation, afraid that if she did not have the railing to lead her back, she might become irrevocably lost in the labyrinth of the broken ships. She kept her hand on the railing and continued farther into the gathered ruins of the ships.

Jonas stepped carefully behind her over floorboards that occasionally lay shattered beneath their feet. With each passing moment, more memories of their life together in the world . . . itself a strange thought . . . grew clearer in her mind. The impression she had was that it had been a difficult life made somehow stronger and more meaningful, she thought, by the tragedies they had endured together. That life had forged a bond between them that she was only now beginning to understand and even appreciate. Yet wasn't he responsible for her separation from Jenny in the first place? Hadn't he selfishly and obsessively waited for her at the Gate only to pull her into a mortal life that she had not chosen for herself? She was uncertain, now that she knew what he had done, whether he was acting in their mutual interests or primarily on his own.

"What is this place, Ellis?" Jonas stepped softly behind her with an amazed Margaret and a rather fearful Alicia trailing behind.

"I don't know exactly," Ellis replied.

"But milady created it, did you not?" Margaret spoke as though it were both an assertion and a question all at once.

"I believe I did, after a fashion," Ellis commented as she turned the corner at an intersection of hallways into another passage identical to the one they had just left. It was increasingly apparent that they were in some form of a maze.

"But this is madness," Jonas said. "You've never been in such a place and I doubt very much if you have ever even imagined anything like this."

"You're asking me what rules I'm following." Ellis smiled to herself at the thought that Jonas did not understand the nature of the place he had taken her from a lifetime ago.

"Yes." Jonas nodded. "I suppose I am."

"Well, I hardly know them myself although given what I've learned of my life here before, I must have been rather adept at them in the past." Ellis came to another intersection and led them to the right this time. "I don't try to form a place with my thoughts so much as a purpose. It feels easier to let the exact form follow its own direction than to try and force every detail. The Tween seems to conform to our hearts rather than our minds on a level deeper and more complete than conscious thought. It then presents the Day in whatever form that will be the most meaningful to whoever's Day it represents."

"I thought Merrick created this Day," Alicia said from the back of the group.

"Merrick was rushed into using a Book of the Day that was not his own." Ellis came to another side corridor and considered it for a moment, then continued straight ahead. "It *is* still Merrick's Day . . ."

"But it was *your* Book!" Margaret said in wondrous delight.

"Exactly," Ellis agreed as they approached a turn in the corridor.

"So you have some say in the formation of Echo House even if it isn't your Day?" Alicia was so shocked by this thought that she momentarily forgot their terrible surroundings.

"Yes, it appears that I do." Ellis nodded.

"But that's cheating!" Alicia exclaimed.

"No, just more rules; my rules, it would seem," Ellis corrected. "Make no mistake, however, this is *still* very much Merrick's Day. I've been able to change some of the places in Echo House into places that seem to serve our purposes although, in truth, the forms sometimes make no sense to me."

"Nor to me," Jonas said, pointing ahead of them as they turned the corner in another corridor. "But it seems we have arrived somewhere."

The double doors before them were fitted with panes of frosted glass etched in an art nouveau stylizing of a woman stepping out of a well with a scourge in one hand and a mirror in the other. Words arched over the figure read *Vérité sortant du puits armée de son martinet pour châtier l'humanité.*

"Whatever is that supposed to mean?" Alicia demanded.

"It means 'Truth rises out of her well to shame mankind,'" Ellis translated for the shaking woman. "What do you say to us rising out of the well?"

Ellis reached forward with both hands, grasped both door handles and pushed both doors open wide. She stepped in with Jonas just behind her. Alicia clung to Margaret's arm with a viselike grip despite the best efforts of the lady's maid to extract herself. As they stepped into the room, the doors quietly shut behind them.

It looked as though the hulls of seven enormous ships had been gutted and turned on their end to form a single monstrous room. The keels all rose to meet overhead at their bows, creating a domed roof fifty feet over their heads. The timbers that formed the horizontal ribs were exposed, marching upward from the scrubbed planks of a fitted hardwood floor beneath Ellis's feet. The entire space was harshly lit by numerous electric chandeliers that hung suspended from the keels of each hull.

There between each keel and set upon the horizontal rib beams were books.

Thousands of books.

Books filled every niche between the ribs, their courses rising nearly to the very peak of the room.

To one side of the impossible library, a ridiculously tall ladder stood against one of the book stacks. Atop it, a single figure sat, its back against the books as it perched on the uppermost rung. Its long claws were black and sharp, struggling to maintain its grip on the book into which its face was buried. But the hands were brick red as were its arms where they were exposed beneath the rolled-up sleeves of its white shirt and the torn gray waistcoat whose buttons were undone. The man's trousers were torn open and shredded at the knees, exposing sinewy legs matching the same brick red of its hands and ending in cloven hooves as black as its claws. A twisting tail of the same color wrapped around one of the legs of the ladder between its rungs, its bone-barbed end flicking listlessly as the creature buried its face in the book.

Alicia released Margaret, cowering at once against the closed door.

"Ellis, I think we need to leave." There was an urgency in Jonas's whisper.

"Not at all," Ellis replied in a clear, strong voice that echoed back toward her from the dome overhead.

Margaret winced at the loudness of the sound in so quiet a space.

"We've only just arrived here and would not wish to offend our host." Ellis turned around, her face rising toward where the demonic creature remained with its face buried in its book. "And we certainly would not wish to offend our host, would we, Dr. Carmichael?"

The demon perched atop the ladder lowered his book suddenly and stared down at Ellis. His face was now more angular than she remembered and his skin tone now matched the deep red of the rest of him. His eyes were an uncomfortable yellow color with a reptile-like slit instead of the expected pupil. The ears were distinctly pointed. Still, despite it all, Ellis recognized the general features of the creature and the wild shock of white hair he preferred combed backward from the forehead between two sharp horns protruding from his head.

There was no denying that the demon atop the ladder was Dr. Carmichael.

"Ah, Miss Ellis." The demon smiled back at her with sharp, pointed teeth though there was venom in his eyes. "What a delight to see you again . . . goodbye and go away."

The demon Carmichael returned again to perusing the book.

"We've come calling," Ellis insisted.

"Not taking visitors, Miss Ellis," Carmichael called back from behind his book. "I am distinctly not at home!"

"That's Dr. Carmichael?" Alicia screeched. "What happened to him?"

"Ah, Alicia Van der Meer, I see that you are as astute and quick-witted as ever," Carmichael sneered as he slammed closed the book and gazed down from his perch. "What happened to me, indeed? Perhaps you could ask your friend, Miss Ellis Harkington, how it is that I appear in such a state?"

"Why should we ask her?" Margaret insisted. "What has she to do with the likes of you?"

"The *likes* of me?" Carmichael howled in sudden rage. The demon threw the book in anger from the top of the ladder, slamming it into the books on the opposite wall and causing a minor cascade of volumes. He leaped from the top rung, causing the ladder to shift dangerously.

Ellis and Jonas took several hasty steps back as Carmichael plunged toward the floor. Suddenly, leathery wings
unfolded from the torn back of the demon's waistcoat, arresting his fall just before he hit the ground. Carmichael
crouched from the impact and then stood before them,
his wings quivering in his rage behind him as he faced
Margaret, who had hastily retreated against a stack of
books.

"The likes of me is *exactly* why I look this way!" Carmichael shouted. He turned to face Ellis. "You did this
to me!"

"I did no such thing!" Ellis stood her ground, indignation evident in her expression.

"You did exactly that!" Carmichael seethed, his wings
still rustling behind him. He turned to Alicia, still pressed
against the door. "Tell me, Miss Van der Meer, just whom
were you expecting to find?"

"We've come for Jenny," Jonas said, trying to inter-
ject himself between Carmichael and the costumed girl.

Carmichael ignored him. "And just how did you expect
to find Jenny?"

"Well." Alicia was hesitant. "Ellis said the angels
wouldn't help us so we needed to find . . ."

Alicia's eyes went wide.

Lucian Carmichael took a step back, taking care of his
own barbed tail as he bowed deeply, pain still registering
in his eyes.

"Just so, a demon." Lucian completed the thought in

his own words. "That's how her 'ladyship' Ellis sees me and that's how I must appear in this pointless charade. At your service . . . and leave me alone, I want no part of you."

Carmichael turned on his cloven foot and began walking away back toward where the book he had thrown had fallen. His wings dragged slightly behind him.

"You can help us," Ellis called to him.

"Ah, if only I cared," he called back over his shoulder.

"We can help you in turn," Ellis tried again.

"Don't care." Lucian did not bother to even glance back as he spoke. He reached down and picked up the book again. "Nobody home. Don't need anything you're selling."

"But you're looking for something, too," Jonas offered, stepping forward. "Here in the books. Something you haven't found yet."

"Very clever, sir, and I'll bet you thought that up all on your own." Carmichael continued picking up the fallen books, examining them and then setting them aside.

"You're looking for the way out, aren't you?" Jonas pressed.

"So what if I am." The demon shrugged.

Ellis raised her chin, suddenly understanding. "But you're not just looking for *any* way out. You're a demon. You inherently know where the Gate is back to your own infernal regions. But that's not the Gate you're interested in finding."

"You've changed your mind, haven't you?" Jonas said. "You don't want the demon's Gate, you want to—"

"And how do you think I'll be able to get through the Gate looking like this?" Carmichael replied angrily. "What angel is going to convince the Sentinels that I'm done with the old ways? When I show up with everything but a pitchfork?"

"Why would you even want to try?" Jonas asked. "You aren't of the Tween; already chose the darkness. Why not just return through your own gateway back to the hell that sent you?"

"Because I can't go back," the doctor snapped.

"Why not?"

"Because I was lousy at my job!" Dr. Carmichael shouted. "They don't want me back. They say that I've become too attached to the idea of Earth and seduced by the promise of mortality. I was supposed to come here and convert the souls of the Tween into choosing mandated order and instead, it seems, they've converted me into doubting my own choice."

"What?" Jonas scoffed. "A reformed devil?"

"You ever read Heraclitus, boy?" Carmichael's words were bitter. "He said change is the only constant. We all change or we rot. And, yes, just knowing about Heraclitus seems to call my commitment to my former masters into question. So I'm looking for a better offer from a, shall we say, more forgiving group. But how can I do that looking like *this*?"

"Jonas will help you," Ellis said, wondering if she had just lied to the demon.

"I can," Jonas replied. "I will."

Carmichael stood still, his breathing laboring against his emotions. It took him long moments before he managed to speak. "You . . . you just had to come back, didn't you, Ellis? Why did you come back? I thought if I could learn about your life and what it was like to breathe and love and hate and have pain and joy that it would be enough. Why did you have to come back and show me what I was lacking? Why did you give me a taste for things I could never have?"

"Jenny trusted you," Ellis said. "She would have come to you first for help when Merrick changed the Day."

"Leave me alone." The demon breathed the words out between his sharp teeth.

"Where's Jenny, Lucian?" Ellis asked quietly.

Carmichael looked away.

"We can help you but you've got to help us first." Ellis's voice was soft as she spoke. "She's here, isn't she, Lucian?"

"Yes," the demon replied in a whisper that she could barely hear.

"Show me where she is, Lucian," Ellis said, steadying her voice to a calm she did not feel.

The demon reached down to the stack of fallen books at his feet. Ellis had not realized it before now but all of the books in this library were scrapbooks, as though all of the collected scrapbooks of each soul in the Tween had been gathered here to one place. Carmichael pushed several aside before lifting up a single tome, the cover of which was unadorned. He turned toward Ellis and handed her the book.

"Here," he said.

Ellis took the scrapbook and examined it. Most scrapbooks she had found here were intricately adorned but this one was very simple. The cover was in blue dyed suede leather with a dull bronze binding on the spine.

Ellis moved to open the book but the demon's red, clawed hand came down gently on her own to prevent her.

"Remember, Ellis," Carmichael said. "Sometimes the only way back is forward."

Ellis gave the demon a quizzical look as he stepped back.

"Ellis," Jonas said in sudden alarm. "Wait!"

She opened the book.

She felt a sudden pull forward. The book suddenly grew in size or perhaps she was getting smaller. All she knew was that she was being pulled between the pages and into the binding.

In the next moment, Ellis vanished from the library.

20

THE BLANK PAGE

For a moment, Ellis felt disoriented.

She stood in her green traveling dress in the middle of a featureless white plain. Her feet were firmly planted against the dull white surface but it seemed to extend away from her toward no discernable horizon. The sky above was white, too; she assumed everywhere was the same featureless blank.

Ellis recalled having once been in a heavy snowfall in Boston when she was in her high school years. She could see nothing beyond the blank whiteness around her. The sunlight was so completely diffused by the clouds and snow that not even its brightness could be discerned overhead. She remembered it as being both disconcerting and comforting at the same time, as though one could walk anonymously through the falling snow and be sequestered from the world. This place, wherever it was, had much that same feeling about it: the interior of a cocoon.

Ellis stooped down to touch the ground at her feet. As she ran her bare fingers across the surface she felt the slight roughness in the surface of its barely perceptible texture, yet it, too, was familiar to her.

"Paper," she said aloud. The words sounded flat in her ears as though they were absorbed completely by the eternal space around her.

A sigh.

Ellis looked up sharply toward the sound.

There, in the distance, was something after all. It was a slightly darkened blotch at what Ellis could only assume was the horizon of this place. It was blurry and indistinct but at least it was something, a fixed mark that she could find her way toward.

Ellis walked toward the blemish. Whether she walked for minutes or hours she could not tell. The dark blotch grew with every passing step. It began to take on the aspects of a watercolor done in shades of green and blue. The edges of the colors had bloomed together as though flowing through fibers in the paper from a brush that was too wet. It was not just beneath her but it also seemed to flow around her at the sides and above as well, staining the stark whiteness in its soft, colorful haze.

With every step, more definition came into the painting that flowed about her. Above, the watercolor became a more distinctive blue with patches of white while the greens became more separated and varied in their sweeping shapes. Some congealed into blotches of individual leaves and long sweeping swaths of color reminiscent of tall grass. Soon browns, blacks and yellows appeared.

A brownish path formed beneath her feet. It meandered amid tall blades of grass formed of swaths of color more pronounced and with sharper edges than before. The blue of the sky congealed, retreating from where white clouds took form. Trees emerged from the blurred green shades, their trunks, branches and leaves growing more distinct with every step that she took. Soon the woods surrounded her on the path, the trees arching overhead, and the light from the sky shining down through the leaves dappled her form as she continued to follow the trail wandering before her. She recalled that she had come down this same trail before, sometime deep in her past.

The pathway emerged from the woods into a small meadow. It continued across the soft grasses to the far side of the clearing where a familiar wall stood. It was rendered, Ellis thought to herself, in the mixed media of watercolors and pencils.

In the wall at the end of the path was a gate.

Not *the* Gate, she reminded herself. This, too, was drawn in the same manner as the walls and surrounding foliage but it nevertheless was a perfect likeness of the Gate out of the Tween through which she had somehow passed seemingly an eternity before.

There, sitting next to the trail in the soft grasses and

surrounded by flowers, sat the familiar form for whom
Ellis had sought so diligently.

"Jenny," Ellis breathed.

Her cousin looked up and smiled.

"You're . . . you're changed," Ellis said.

Jenny's bobbed hair was now long and luxuriously
styled up onto her head. She was the picture of a Gibson
girl and, judging by the sharpness of her appearance, the
only thing truly real in the scene that had materialized
before Ellis. She wore an old-fashioned dress of white
linen and lace, complete with large leg-of-mutton sleeves.
Her curls were carefully coiffed up off the shoulders. The
skirt was splayed carefully about her on a picnic blanket
that shielded her from the grass.

"Not entirely changed, my dear Ellis," Jenny answered.
She held up her gloved hands, which appeared more de-
formed and contorted than Ellis recalled them. Still, her
smile at Ellis's approach was radiant.

Ellis shook her head in puzzlement. "But your hair . . .
the dress . . ."

"Ellis," she answered, the sound of the name filled
with sunshine. "I knew you would come back to me, if
I waited long enough."

"Like Jonas," Ellis acknowledged, then she glanced at
her cousin's hands. "But not entirely. Was it painful?"

"Was what painful?"

"The Gate . . . when it closed."

Jenny's smile dimmed. "Yes. It was painful. I don't

remember much about it, to be completely honest. I believe Alicia was here at the time. She got me back to Gamin somehow and to Uncle Lucian's office. Uncle said that it was not unusual for someone who has had such trauma to not remember it clearly. He took care of me for quite some time after . . . after the accident."

Jenny looked down at her own hands, twisted in her lap.

"Do you remember that day, Ellis? Do you know what happened?"

"I remember." Ellis nodded. "That is how I knew where to find you."

"And so you have!" Jenny brightened at the thought. "You came back for me as I always knew that you would. Now we can be safe here together, just you and I!"

Ellis stepped carefully across the painted meadow. Flowers and blades of grass became more real wherever she stepped. "I came back for you, Jenny, but I didn't come to stay."

"Why not?" Jenny's smile fell a bit at the corners.

"Because we have to leave, Jenny."

Ellis offered her hand.

"No. No we don't." Jenny withdrew slightly. "You've come back to me, as I knew you would. No one else could find me here. No one else could know where to look. We can be safe here. I knew if I waited, you would come and everything could go back to the way that it was before."

"No, Jenny," Ellis sighed. "We cannot go back."

"Perhaps you don't remember," Jenny continued, desperation rising in her voice. "But I know how it used to be with us. We can start over in this place—fresh and new."

"Tabula rasa?" Ellis asked.

"Exactly! A blank slate!" Jenny replied, reaching out with her twisted hands toward Ellis. "We start over here, just the two of us at the Gate where we were separated. Only this time we won't let anyone else in. We can build a Day of our own, just the two of us right here, and make it into whatever we wanted. No one could find us! It would just be you and me, here in our own little world where no one could hurt us or make us afraid. We could be safe here, you and I."

"Oh, my dear Jenny." Ellis looked on her cousin with a sad smile.

"But isn't that a wonderful dream?" Jenny pleaded.

"Yes, Jenny, it is." Ellis drew in a deep breath. "That is such a wonderful dream. To be able to stay asleep forever where there is no pain, no suffering and no evil. There is a part of me that wishes that we could just turn our backs on it all . . . the madness, hurt, cruelty, ignorance . . . and just retreat into ourselves."

"Then let's do it," Jenny begged. "Together we could . . . what's wrong?"

Ellis knelt down on the blanket with her cousin, folding Jenny's crippled hands into her own.

"We cannot stay," Ellis said.

"Of course we can," Jenny begged. "You just said . . ."

"I said it was a wonderful dream." Ellis spoke softly. "But it is only a dream and we cannot live here."

"Why not?" Jenny was on the verge of tears.

"Because I've been to the world, Jenny," Ellis said as gently as she could. "Because I've brought the world with me. It's part of me, part of my memories and part of who I am. We have to go back because neither of us can really hope to have joy without understanding despair, or appreciate health without sickness or feel pleasure without knowing pain, too. We cannot hide from it any longer, Jenny. We have to choose."

"Choose?" Jenny said. "But you said that we didn't have to choose—that we could stay here and be content forever."

"I was . . . I was wrong, Jenny." Ellis looked into Jenny's eyes, hoping she would understand. "I didn't understand that one cannot have contentment without knowing restlessness or anxiety. Life is more than just breath. We do not just choose to live . . . we live because we choose."

"I don't understand," Jenny said, tears welling from her eyes.

"But I do understand, Jenny," Ellis said as she stood up, eyeing the gate. "Because I remember what happened at the Gate."

•   •   •

The old gate is high and heavy and hidden
Till you choose to be chosen it is forbidden

The toll for passage is the age of a man
You cannot go back the way you began.
What am I?

She had found the Gate at last. Her rage against Merrick was such that she had determined to flee as far from him as she could go but she was surprised to find just how far she had come. The Day was changing, this time to Merrick's Day, and she had been angry at having lost the Day to him, no matter how briefly. Now they were in the twilight of the Day, shifting from one to the next, and everything had lost any semblance of form or nature until the Day took on the shape of Merrick's will.

Only the Gate remained.

She was suddenly filled with curiosity. The bothersome Messengers had spoken of what awaited them beyond the Gate—a place she had laughingly called the "Garden of Wonders." But now she wanted to know just what it was that lay beyond the Gate.

But how?

That was the question in her mind. To pass the Gate was to choose and once chosen the Gate would close, forever barring their return. Yet she had no intention of choosing; she only wished to satisfy her curiosity as to what lay beyond the Gate.

She might not be able to choose, she realized, but perhaps she did not have to do so.

She would open the Gate but not pass fully through

it. She would keep one foot in Gamin and the other just barely within the Garden of Wonders.

She would cheat the Gate.

She knew that she needed to hurry. Alicia had been following her and she did not wish for her to interfere. She stepped up to the Gate, pushed it open and leaned through its casement.

It was filled with light but in the light she discerned two beings. One stood watch on the other side of the Gate, a glorious, magnificent Guardian. The other sat nearby and stood at once at the opening of the Gate.

To her astonishment, she knew him.

He had waited for her on the distant side of the Gate.

He rushed toward her.

She wanted to speak with him, curious as to why he had remained there.

She wanted to stay in the Tween.

The Gate closed on her indecision.

It severed her soul in twain, tearing one desire from the other. She saw the Gate close on what remained of her frightened self, her hands caught in the Gate as they reached for her curious self.

Her half-soul collapsed in the Garden of Wonders. She was barely aware of the voices speaking over her.

"She cannot stay." It was the One Who Waited by the Gate.

"She cannot go back." It was the Guardian by the Gate.

"I will take her then."

"Where will you take her?"

"Where she can become strong again."

"And what of you?"

"I will go, too."

"I came back for you, Jenny," Ellis said. "You're the reason I returned. Neither of us will ever be whole without the other."

Jenny stared at Ellis, struggling to comprehend. "If . . . if what you say is true, then where do we go from here?"

"We go back," Ellis said.

"Through the Gate?" Jenny's voice quivered as she spoke.

"Yes, I believe so."

"And if we do . . . where will it take us?"

"I don't know, Jenny," Ellis said. "But wherever it leads us, I believe we'll be whole . . . you and I. Wherever that is, it will be home."

Jenny bowed her head, offering her withered hand to Ellis.

"Then take us home," she said.

Jenny began to weep, her tears striking the water-colored paper, causing the colors to blossom and smear. In answer, a gentle rain of teardrops started to fall around them, further blurring the colors and washing them away. The garden and the gate faded away as did the blur of color, too, as the paper world around them grew whiter, clearer and cleaner.

Ellis stood, staring at the blank page of the scrapbook in front of her. She held up the book on the right side while a smaller, withered hand in gloves struggled to hold up the left.

Ellis and Jenny stood side by side before one of the bookcases of Lucian's library.

Ellis sighed with relief. "Jonas! We've got to hurry and—"

"Oh, there's no hurry, your ladyship."

Ellis spun around toward the voice.

"That which was lost is now found."

Mrs. Crow smiled back at her.

As did Merrick.

21

MARGARET'S DAY

Ellis pulled Jenny with her back against the book-shelves, her eyes searching desperately about the library. It had grown suddenly darker, shadows filling the upper reaches of the stacks along the octagonal perimeter of the room and extending up into the dome overhead, blocking out all light from above. The Shades shifted, thick and palpable overhead in the vague shapes of long-limbed creatures with talons for fingers and embers for eyes.

Yet it was Mrs. Crow that Ellis found the most terrifying of all. The glint in the elderly woman's eyes had turned decidedly wicked. The curl playing at the edge of her narrow smile reminded her of a little girl she once knew who took pleasure in tearing the wings off of butterflies. And more than all of that was one observation that truly chilled her to the bone.

Merrick was sweating.

He feared Mrs. Crow.

As, apparently, did both Margaret and Alicia. Margaret stood to one side of the room, her back pressed against one of the bookcases, trying hard not to be noticed. Alicia stood just slightly behind Merrick, peering around his jacket back at Ellis and Jenny.

Dr. Carmichael lay in his devilish form, his boney arms raised protectively in front of his face as he cowered against the polished stone floor in front of Ellis.

Jonas was nowhere in sight.

"I am most grateful to you, your ladyship," Mrs. Crow said. She took deliberate, calculated steps across the floor, the hard soles of her shoes clacking against the stone with each step. "Even I, a person of great faith, began to doubt that I would ever manage success in this place."

"Faith?" Ellis drew in a breath. "What kind of church professes your faith?"

"Surely someone of your upbringing and high station in life knows that faith has nothing to do with a church," Mrs. Crow sneered. "One can have faith in order and punishment. One can have faith in cloaking darkness. One can certainly—oh most certainly—have faith in vengeance."

"So you found us," Ellis replied.

"Thanks in no small part to Alicia's help," Mrs. Crow

said with a nod toward the girl cowering at Merrick's back. "To your credit, Lady Ellis, the price of her betrayal was a good deal steeper than the traditional—what do you call it—thirty pieces of silver, but nevertheless a bargain."

Ellis shot an accusing glance at Alicia, then glared at the malevolent housekeeper. "I suppose this means you've won the Day."

Mrs. Crow stopped and chuckled.

"You find me amusing?" Ellis demanded as she struggled to remain calm.

"Oh, I couldn't care less about the Day." Mrs. Crow shrugged with a dismissive wave of her hand.

"Then why look for us at all?"

"You?" Mrs. Crow chortled. "I wasn't looking for *you* at all!"

Her gaze fell on the red-brick form of Dr. Carmichael, whimpering on the floor.

"Him?"

"Oh, yes, him: Dr. Lucian Carmichael." Mrs. Crow spat the name through clenched teeth. "You had a service to perform, didn't you, Lucian? A calling from the Prince in Exile to garner more souls to his rightful cause. You came here at his bidding because he *believed* in you. And how did you repay that trust?"

"No," Carmichael pleaded, his cloven hooves scraping against the floor as he tried to push himself away. "You don't understand what it's like here . . . what I've had to do!"

"Oh, I believe I understand perfectly," Mrs. Crow continued, baring her teeth. "You saw the pretty shadows of mortality, the children playing at life. You got a taste for, if you'll pardon the expression, well, the idea of taste . . . and smell and sight and touch. You found it easy to forget why you had come here, what was expected of you by the Prince in Exile and your duty. You were meant to be a powerful seduction for our cause, and what did you become? A demon with a daiquiri? Beelzebub in a boater hat?"

Ellis noticed the Shades lurking around the edge of the dome began slowly to descend. The air became palpably colder as they approached.

She pushed Jenny gently behind her, glancing about the room. The exit was on the opposite side from where they stood. Margaret stood pressed against the bookcase to one side. Alicia, Merrick, Mrs. Crow and all the Shades were between her and the door.

"There's got to be another way out," Ellis muttered to herself. "Think! Think of another way out!"

"Please, don't make me go back. Not now," Carmichael begged. The horns of his head were nearly at Ellis's feet. "I . . . I've seen too much. Learned too much! Just leave me behind, say you never found me. It's for your own sake, you know. I'd be a terrible, infecting presence in the Prince's realm!"

"No, I don't think so." Mrs. Crow stood over him, the Shades closing in around them. Ellis could feel not just cold but the complete absence of warmth. "In fact, I don't think you'll be anything at all."

Ellis tried to draw in a breath.

In an instant, the glass of the overhead dome shattered to dust with a crash.

The Shades' screams pierced Ellis, running through her head with painful intensity.

Light exploded into the library from above. Ellis was momentarily blinded by its intensity. The rush of flapping wings filled the air. Ellis instinctively raised her arms in front of her face, hoping it would shield her against whatever new horror was raining down around her. She turned, pressing against Jenny, trying to shield her as well.

"Ellis!"

Jonas. Jonas's voice.

She turned and opened her eyes. Jonas was rushing toward her around the edge of the library floor. He was just passing Margaret as Ellis looked up.

The air was still glittering with the glass particles whirling about the rotunda, driven into the air by the flapping of enormous wings of brilliant white.

"Angels," Ellis breathed. "My angels."

The bright, winged forms of beauty swung, bounded and soared about the rotunda, their brilliance muted and shuttered by the figures of the Shades that were devoid of light. They pursued each other about the open space, light crashing into darkness and darkness tearing at the light in turn. Each fought desperately to contain the other, bind it against its will and prevent its dominance in the room. One of the Shades was successfully bound only to be released by another.

Beneath the raging battle overhead, Mrs. Crow uttered an anguished, angry cry. Leathery wings erupted from her back, tearing the cloth of the dress as they unfolded. Her plump, rosy cheeks grew sunken and sallow. The white hair of her head tore loose from its restraint, writhing about her head in snaky tendrils. The fingers of her hands elongated into talons as she turned again to face Carmichael.

"Now!" Jonas shouted, pulling at Ellis's arm. "Come on!"

Ellis grasped Jenny's thin arm in turn, following Jonas's lead around the edge of the room. Margaret watched them from the opposite side, her gaze untroubled and somehow knowing. Ellis did not pause, but continued around the library rotunda, the door now only a few steps away.

Merrick shoved Alicia to the side as he stepped back into the doorway, rage quivering his body as he suddenly blocked their way.

"NO!" he shouted.

The angels and the Shades suddenly slowed in their flight, coming to a stop in midair. Ellis's Soldiers were still bright with light but she could see now that they still wore the uniforms she had pictured them in when she had encountered them in the hospital. Their beautiful, feathered wings of white were outstretched as they hung suspended in the air. So, too, it was with the Shades, parts of whom she could now see more clearly than she had before. The hands were identical to the transformed Mrs. Crow—long with talons—and each head was covered in a distinctive cowl trimmed in intricate ornamentation. Though the faces remained uncomfortably out of focus the eyes were shining pinpricks of blackness visible only when they looked directly at the observer. The particles of glass were suspended in the air, glinting at Ellis as she haltingly stopped. Even Mrs. Crow's gargoyle form and the demonically transformed Dr. Carmichael were fixed as though time no longer moved forward.

"You!" Merrick shouted, his hand extended toward Jonas.

Jonas took a step back in surprise and confusion. "How? How are you doing this?"

"This is MY Day, Jonas!" Merrick screamed as he stepped purposefully forward.

Jonas stumbled backward, pushing Ellis and Jenny against the bookshelves lining the wall. "But you are forbidden from interfering with the Soldiers or the Shades when they—"

Merrick's hand shot out to Jonas's neck. It clamped around his throat, choking off the soldier's voice mid-sentence.

"How dare you bring *war* into my house!" Merrick raged. He lifted Jonas up from the ground with one arm, his grip tight on the man's larynx. "I, who have done so much for these souls, who led them to a place of safety . . . a refuge from your idealistic squabbling and conflict . . . will I permit one heartsick trespasser to bring the war to ME and MY PEOPLE?"

"No, Merrick," Jenny pleaded. "Stop!"

"I haven't yet gotten started!" Merrick railed.

He tossed Jonas through the air as though he were a doll. The young soldier flew toward the center of the library. He held his arms across his face only moments before he dove head-first into the suspended glass particles in the room. Jonas screamed in agony. The glass particles gave way reluctantly, each one raking across his skin, scouring it raw. By the time Jonas slammed against the opposite wall of books, the backs of his hands were bleeding.

Ellis watched as Merrick rounded the outer perimeter of the rotunda, stalking Jonas where he lay. She glanced toward the door, contemplating how she might slip past Merrick, desperate to somehow find help.

The doorway was gone. A bookshelf stood in its place. The exit had vanished. There was no way out.

"Even the Tween has rules you must obey," Jonas choked out between his coughs. He struggled to get his feet back under him. "You cannot stop the Soldiers or the Shades!"

"Oh, I haven't *stopped* them," Merrick sneered. "I've slowed them down is all; slow enough so that everything that happens here will take place between breaths. Time enough for me to banish you to the Umbra!"

"You cannot do it," Jonas said, even as Merrick gathered up the front of his uniform in his hands and dragged him up off of the stained marble floor. "You have no such power over the angels or the demons in the Tween."

"Oh, that's quite true," Merrick said. "But, then, those rules don't actually apply to you, do they?"

Jonas's eyes went wide.

"Leave him alone, Merrick," Ellis demanded.

"But your guide and rescuer has a little secret, Ellis," Merrick continued as he picked Jonas up bodily from the floor by the tunic. "You see, the rules don't actually apply to him. Can you guess why?"

"Because." Ellis drew in her own quick breath. "Because he isn't really that kind of Soldier, is he?"

"He's a sneak and a thief." Merrick nodded. "He waited by the Gate until he saw his chance and then he stole you from me. Then, when you returned, he couldn't just wait by the Gate again. Oh, no. He had to find a way in—any way in—so that he could steal you like the thief he is all over again."

A glint of light from one of the glass particles suspended in the air flashed in Ellis's eye . . . then a second and a third.

"This time I'm sending you to a place from which you can never return," Merrick snarled.

Overhead, a deep sound resonated through the rotunda. Ellis looked up and saw the Umbra.

At its edges it appeared to be a spinning vortex of purple light upon which it was impossible to focus. In its center it was a chilling absence of existence. It was not just black, for black is something, but rather a totality of not being: a space devoid of not just the senses but of time or experience. Its contemplation alone was terrifying.

"No one escapes the Umbra until I say they can be released," Merrick sneered. "And I'll *never* permit you to leave."

"So long as it is your Day," Alicia corrected.

More of the glass particles flashed in the lamplight of the room. Suddenly, the stone tiles beneath Merrick cracked. Tendrils of vines erupted from beneath Merrick, reaching up with astonishing swiftness, entwining his legs.

"What is this?" Merrick demanded, looking at Ellis. "What have you done?"

The vines continued to grow out from between the shattered tiles, thickening around his legs and reaching up his body toward his arms, still holding Jonas suspended in the air.

"You cannot stop me, Ellis," Merrick shouted.

"But I'm not!" Ellis cried out. "It's not me!"

"She's right, Merrick," Alicia said with deadly calm as she stepped around the vines weaving tightly around Merrick. "My help for winning the Day. That was the bargain Mrs. Crow offered me on your behalf. You get Ellis and Jenny, the housekeeper takes Dr. Carmichael away as a trophy to her master and I get to rule the Day. Not even you can break such a bargain, Merrick! It's a founding rule of the Tween; a rule that cannot be broken without sundering the Tween—your precious pretense of existence—with it."

"Alicia," Ellis said with caution in her voice. She could see that Jonas was still struggling against Merrick's grip but was quickly weakening. "Keep the Day. Just let us go."

"Let you go?" Alicia laughed, a maniacal edge in the sound. "Oh, no, my dear Ellis. After all the Games *you* made me play? After an eternity of doing what *you* wanted to do? This is *my* Day."

"You fool!" Merrick said. "I never made such a bargain!"

"You did!" Alicia shot back. "Mrs. Crow said—"

"Mrs. Crow?" Merrick scoffed. "She *lied*!"

Alicia's form grew transparent. Ellis could see particles of her drifting upward, dustlike pieces of her falling upward toward the Umbra overhead.

"No!" Alicia cried as her body dissolved upward into the nothing. "It's *my* Day! *I'm* the one! It's *me*!"

Her last words as she dissolved were still echoing in the hall when another voice spoke.

"No, it's me," said Margaret. The forgotten servant was stepping into the center of the floor as the vines also reached outward, wrapping around the pillars at the perimeter of the room and upward into the dome. The vines began to spring into blossoms, rare and beautiful. "It's *me*!"

She was carrying a Book.

It was the Book of *her* Day.

22

END OF DREAMS

argaret." Ellis's mouth had suddenly gone dry. "Please, what you're trying to do is . . . is more difficult than you know."

"Oh, by all means patronize me, your ladyship!" Margaret laughed in derision. "The great Ellis and her abandoned, lesser half together again to torment their little pet Margaret! Why don't you remind me once more how small and insignificant I am in your grand schemes and elaborate pretense? By all means put me in my place, your ladyship!"

"Argh!" Merrick cried out as the vines tightened around his forearms. He released his grip on Jonas, dropping him onto the broken floor. Jonas stumbled backward over the vines, falling on his back.

"You're in over your head, Margaret," Merrick said

through a predatory grin. The vines wrapped tighter about him, threatening to engulf him.

Her black servant's dress was transforming at the same time as the library. The color shifted into brighter whites and blues, the dress filling out with layers of petticoats.

Margaret's dress was a much older style, Ellis realized. *How long has she been waiting to rule the Day?*

"So ordains the great Merrick!" Margaret sneered. "Ruler of all he surveys. Judge and jury if never quite the executioner. You never did want to get your hands dirty, did you, Merrick? You always played the puppeteer, plucking at everyone else's strings so that they could dirty themselves for you. Well, I'm not dancing for you now, Merrick. I'm not . . ."

Ellis gasped.

Enormous strings, nearly as thick as ropes, extended from both of Margaret's wrists up through the dome of the library. Other similar strings ran from her knees through her dress and from the back of her neck up through the shattered dome as well. They drew taut, lifting Margaret's arms up in front of her as she clutched the Book of her Day between them.

Jonas, struggling to get to his feet, murmured, "Please, I just . . . I just want to take her home!"

"Ellis is right, Margaret. It always seems so easy when it isn't your Day that you're living." Merrick stretched his right hand slightly from the tangle of vines still struggling to encase it. "When your dreams are all that you know, it's best not to let your mind wander."

Merrick flicked his fingers.

The cable strings at Margaret's wrists jumped, jerking her hands upward. Her arms swung in front of her as though she were a life-sized marionette. The Book of her Day nearly fell from her hands as she struggled to retain her hold on it.

Quaking behind Ellis, Jenny whispered urgently in her ear, "What do we do? What can we do?"

Ellis hurriedly took in the library with a more critical eye. The pillars that had formed a colonnade around the rotunda were now almost completely encased in the flowering vines but there were gaps in the garden transformation, places that looked slightly out of focus or incomplete. There was the feeling of an unfinished painting about the room or, she realized, more like an artist was trying to paint on top of a previous work but the original kept bleeding through.

The glint of a glass shard flashed in her eye.

Ellis's eyes went wide.

"Jenny!" There was urgency in her voice. "You've got to hold on to something. Something solid or at least something you believe is solid."

"The vines? Perhaps I could—"

"No! Not the vines. Something more real." Ellis looked about them. "One of the bookcases, perhaps, or a pillar if you can get your arms around it, beneath the vines."

"Why, Ellis? You're frightening me!"

"Because the glass dust is starting to move again," Ellis said. "Merrick slowed everything down but Margaret's taken over the Day. She's never done that before. She hasn't the experience to keep her Day intact, especially with Merrick in the room!"

"What does that mean?"

"It means that we don't have much time," Ellis said. "It means the end of dreams. You've got to hold on, now!"

Jenny frantically pushed her arms beneath the vines of the pillar next to her, wincing in pain at the scraping against her skin.

Ellis took a deep breath to steady herself and then stepped out into the rotunda. The glass dust bit at her face but she came to stand still where Margaret could see her.

"Margaret," Ellis spoke. "Please. You need to let me help you."

"You?" Margaret glared. "This is *my* Day! Why would I possibly want *your* help?"

The glass dust was moving quickly enough now to be noticeable. Its sting was lessening on Ellis's skin but it was the increasing velocity of its motion that worried her.

"It's because this is your Day that you need my help," Ellis replied. "What is it that you want, Margaret? What is it that you want to do with your Day?"

Margaret stared back at her. "What do you mean?"

"What do you want to accomplish in your Day?" Ellis pressed. "What is your Day *about*?"

Margaret drew herself up straight. "Justice!"

"Justice?" Ellis took a tentative step forward. The glass dust was shifting around her. She didn't have much time; none of them did. "Justice for what?"

"Justice for every indignity anyone ever visited on me," Margaret said with satisfaction. "Justice for every other Day since we came to this place. Justice for being unimportant, used and abused in every incarnation of the Day. Now it's *my* turn and I'm going to *fix* all of it."

"But you can't, Margaret," Ellis sighed. She could almost feel the wind of the angel's beating wings drifting across her face like a breeze. "None of us can. The past is done. You can't change it."

"We *can*," Margaret whined. "It's my *Day*. We can do it all over again and make it right!"

"We'd make the same mistakes we made before," Ellis said. "I've looked harder for my own past than anyone, Margaret, and we just can't live there. Life isn't found in the past. Life is found in the here and now. What we chose to be before made us into who we are today but we cannot change that, we can only change what we choose to do right now! Let go of the past, Margaret. I can help you . . . we can help each other . . ."

"NO!" Margaret shouted. "You will *pay* for what you did to me! *Everyone* will *pay*!"

Merrick flicked the fingers of his free hand once more.

The marionette ropes wrapped round Margaret's hands jerked violently upward. The Book of her Day tumbled out of her hands and bounced across the vines away from her.

In a moment, the vines encasing Merrick withered into dry husks. Merrick exploded out of them, scattering the brown limbs and leaves into the shifting glass about them.

Margaret stepped back. The ropes binding her flashed suddenly into flame, then fell to ash. She cried out from the pain of freeing herself and lunged toward her Book. The vines still running across the floor tripped her and she fell on her Book of the Day.

Slowly at first but then with greater rapidity, the angels and Shades in the room continued their eternal combat. Their motions seemed graceful as though they were somehow in a dance of war. Mrs. Crow stretched out the talons of her hands toward Carmichael and he struggled to evade her.

Above it all, the rotating Umbra looked down on them like a sightless, unfeeling eye.

Suddenly the room changed, most of its outer walls and floor shifting away and altering their form, texture and color. There were still columns and bookcases but now they were set on the stage of the theater. The audience was all in their seats, gazing back at them from behind their masks. The angels and Shades dove and soared about each other, locked again in their combat.

The audience applauded wildly, many of them leaping to their feet.

Margaret stood up, the Book of her Day in her hands. She screamed incoherently at Merrick. The walls fell away once more, groaning and cracking under the transformation. The audience tumbled through the air, still cheering with applause.

The room shifted again. They were in the ballroom. The pillars of the library were set about the center of the enormous floor along with most of the bookcases. The *Danse Macabre* played as all the masked audience were transformed, now wearing formal wear and settling onto the floor. Ellis saw her mother wheeling across the floor in time to the music with her dead father in pose.

"Ellis!" Jenny called to her from the base of the pillar she was clinging to nearby. "Please! Help me!"

"Just hold on!" Ellis jumped toward the nearest solid object she could see: a bookcase near her on the dance floor. She hoped it would be enough.

As the battle raged between the angels and Shades, so it raged between Merrick and Margaret.

The room imploded and replaced itself with the folly in the garden now ornamented with bookcases, columns and conflict.

It imploded again to be reorganized once more into the parlor of the Disir sisters. "Would you like some cakes to go with that?" said Minnie Disir with a wide smile.

The room tore itself apart once more, collapsing into

the form of the foyer in Summersend. The swirling Umbra remained above them.

Jonas, managing at last to get his feet under him, rushed toward Merrick. He had the sword from one of the Soldiers in his hand and it gleamed with a bright flame.

Merrick saw his approach. He rolled around the thrust of the blade, closing into Jonas as he trapped the sword with his arm. Jonas struggled to get the blade free but Merrick held Jonas's arm tightly.

"Well, my old friend," Merrick said to Jonas. "It has finally come to this."

"Just let us go, Merrick," Jonas groaned.

"Oh, I'll let you go." Merrick smiled. "You are one problem I can solve right now."

Jonas grew transparent, the dust of his form rising toward the Umbra.

"No!" Ellis shouted. "Merrick! Don't!"

Jonas's tears of regret turned to dust. In moments his form had vanished, its ashes fallen upward into the Umbra.

In that instant, the library exploded into a whirlwind of debris. The air itself was roaring about them, carrying bits and pieces of the structure with it. The prows of several ships appeared flying past in a chaotic tornado. She glimpsed parts of Echo House whirling about her in the madness as the house and its dreams came apart. The angels and the Shades were caught up in the rushing wind, carried into its violent wall. Mrs. Crow quickly wrapped an arm about a pillar that somehow remained standing above the floor. Dr. Carmichael, caught in her grip, flailed about in the sudden storm, buffeted by both the gale and the debris it carried with it.

Ellis gripped the heavy bookcase. The gale was gaining strength as something unusual caught Ellis's eye on the shelf.

"The End of Dreams," she muttered to herself. "The beginning of life."

She snatched the Book off the shelf, let go of the bookcase and tumbled into the chaos.

23

INTO THE STORM

Ellis closed her eyes for a moment against the torrent of sights and sounds tumbling about her. She concentrated within herself, trying not to permit the chaos to overwhelm her.

"Steady, girl," she told herself. "You've done this before. Trust in that. Trust in yourself."

Silence fell with utter and shocking suddenness.

She opened her eyes.

The chaos was still there, the confusion of pieces of past Days, her own memories and the hopes of the souls caught in the Tween all roiling about her in complete quiet as each vied for dominance in existence. Everything rushed about her as though tumbling in a gray fog, flashing occasionally with lightning through the darker patches. Everything moved in and out of existence. A piece of banister from Summersend, the doll from her earliest child-hood memory, the doors to the Nightbirds Society, the Disir sisters' moldering cake, the dress from her coming-out party and Jonas's military jacket from when he met her on leave all roared about her flashing into and fading from reality amid a tumult of costumed spirits still clad in their masquerade masks.

There below was Merrick, screaming in rage against the fall of Echo House, his ferocity directed at the fates and most particularly Margaret who had brought about this collapse blinding him to all reason.

Margaret, too, was there, higher in the storm of bro-ken dreams desperately fighting Merrick for control of the Day, knowing that if she failed now, Merrick's wrath and vengeance would be without measure.

Ellis turned her back on them both and gripped her Book more tightly. She was looking for something of her own amid the collapse of reason, something she could use as an anchor in the madness.

As if at her will, it emerged before her. It was not much—only a fragment—but she knew it would be enough.

It was a fragment of a ship broken from the bow.

In careful letters it proclaimed the name *Mary Celeste*.

Ellis reached out with her free hand and gripped the piece of broken top rail above the lettering.

Fragments and splinters of wood began swarming about her, drawn somehow to the order of her will. Pieces of the railing cracked into place, their sound the first she had heard since silence had descended on the chaos.

Sound returned with a vengeance. The storm of shattered dreams now howled at her with the fury of a nor'easter. The timbers of the ship crashed into place with deafening finality, forming the ribs of the hull against which the planks slammed in a cacophony of sound. Three sections of the bowsprit sprang into place, mending the fibers of their splintered wood with a crunch. Ropes, cables and stays whipped through the air, lashing themselves in place as the masts drove downward through the reassembled deck. The strips of tattered sails wove themselves together out of the fog. The ship was reassembling itself as though in the reverse of an explosion, pulling itself back together from its shattered remains to become whole once more.

Ellis swung over the side and planted her feet upon the reconstituted deck as the gathering ship sailed through the ferocity of the chaotic tempest still raging about her. Driving rain began to pelt her face as she gripped a backstay for support, facing the bow. The wind rushed at her from out of the chaos and tried to drown her as well as her words but she would not be denied.

"I *choose*," she screamed into the storm. "I *choose*!"

"I *choose*," sobbed Ellis as the ship around her shifted form and the sky became painfully bright.

This time the memory was fresh and clear. She was standing again on the deck of the schooner *Lola R*. She was making her way out of the harbor in the passage between Summersend and the lighthouse on Curtis Island. The expanse of Penobscot Bay and the Atlantic Ocean lay beyond. It was midmorning on a chill October day but she wanted to stand on the deck despite the biting wind.

"Are you sure, Ellie?"

The voice was warm in her ear as he wrapped his arms around her from behind.

She sank backward into his embrace though her eyes remained fixed on the old house by the sea that she now thought of as home.

"Yes, Jonas, I'm sure," she heard herself say, and knew that she meant it with all her heart. "I suppose I love this place more than about anywhere else in the world. But after losing you, I realized that I loved it *because* it was where I found you again."

"You found me?" Jonas chuckled. He was wearing his heavy long coat over his uniform but she felt comfortable in his arms. "I thought I was the one who found you here!"

"Maybe we found each other," Ellis chuckled. "Can you at least concede that much?"

"As you wish." Jonas smiled. They were passing the lighthouse now, the sweep of its great eye shuttered during the day. "You'll like Halifax. There is a real need for nurses there and as an army engineer we'll see a lot of each other until I'm shipped out. And when all of this is over, Ellis, I promise, we can find each other again."

"Here?" Ellis purred. "Let it be here at Summersend."

"Of course," Jonas agreed. "If that's where you choose."

"I do choose," Ellis said, turning her back on Summersend at last and facing him. Her hands rose to his back and she pulled him close.

She sighed into his coat. "I do choose . . . I choose . . ."

". . . you."

Ellis wept the word into a peaceful, breaking dawn.

Ellis realized she was standing at the bow clinging to the backstay, now facing a new and breaking day. She blinked through her sudden tears.

She now stood on the foredeck of the *Mary Celeste* as it sailed across a gentle sea. There was only a slight swell, which the ship took easily as it bounded through the waters. She could hear the hush sound as the bow broke through the water beneath her. The gentle rustle of the sails behind her murmured comfort in her ears. Off the larboard beam—she smiled at the memory of her father teaching her the old nautical term for directly off the left side of the ship—there was a terrible storm, ink black at the horizon cut through occasionally with flashes of lightning.

The clouds of that storm billowed dark and menacingly into the sky, but in the distance forward off the bow she could see the faintest line of a sunrise beckoning her toward clearing skies.

We've outrun the storm, Ellis thought. *We'll make it home.*

"Welcome back, Ellis," said a young man's voice behind her.

Ellis turned expectantly but her face fell when she recognized him. "Silenus? However did you get here?"

"I was going to ask you the same question," Silenus Tune replied. He was wearing the same suit she remembered seeing him in when they had first met in the Nightbirds Society. "I heard you call me here . . . so I came. We all did."

Silenus gestured back aft down the deck of the ship. Past the hatch covers toward the quarterdeck, Ellis was relieved to see Jenny, leaning slightly over the rail so that she might see what lay on their course ahead. The following wind blew about a few wisps of her hair that had escaped the tight bun at the back of her head and she seemed delighted at the freshening sea air.

Beyond her, Dr. Carmichael clung to the ladder leading back to the quarterdeck. He had lost the demonic brick-red skin tones, the horns, tail and cloven feet. He again appeared as she had first met him in the guise of her uncle. He had managed to retain his boater hat. Nevertheless there was a sad cast to his eyes that she did not remember before and he seemed ill at ease despite the serene passage of the vessel over the gentle sea.

On the quarterdeck, as she expected, stood Captain Walker at the helm. As she was pulling the ship together from the carnage about her, it occurred to her that they would need a seaman familiar with the operation of the craft. His face still carried the countenance of a hound dog but his eyes were brighter and he stood taller on the deck, his hands wrapped comfortably around the handles of the ship's wheel.

Next to him stood Ely Rossini, his face more peaceful than Ellis ever remembered seeing it.

"Let go and haul, if you please, Dr. Carmichael," Captain Walker called down the length of the deck in a booming voice.

"I should be delighted to assist," the doctor groused, "if I had any idea what you just said."

Ellis frowned. "Why is Lucian here?"

"Only you can answer that, Ellis." Silenus smiled. He turned away, calling back to the doctor. "He means we're on the best course for this wind and we need to trim the sails accordingly."

"And just how am I supposed to do that?" the doctor shot back.

"I'll come and show you," Silenus said.

"Wait, Silenus," Ellis said, putting her hand lightly on his arm to detain him.

"What is it, Ellis?"

"Is this all?"

"All what?"

"All that followed me," Ellis murmured. "I called to so many from the chaos, offered them a place to come."

"Don't blame them, Ellis. They were afraid," Silenus said. "Afraid of Merrick. Afraid of you. More afraid of where you were going, maybe. But you managed to salvage the Day after all before we all fell into the Umbra. Surely, the souls of the Tween must be grateful to you for that."

"What happened to them?" Ellis asked, genuinely concerned.

"I can't answer for all of them but I can show you some," Silenus said with a smile. He reached behind him and pulled around a hard, leather tube that had been slung on his back. The young man quickly undid the latch and removed a beautiful brass telescope. He pulled it open to its full length, put it up to his eye and then handed it to Ellis as he pointed. "There. About two points to starboard of where Captain Walker stands."

Ellis picked up the telescope and raised it to her eye. Her view skittered along the horizon until she centered on the dark form in the distance of their wake. It was a brig not unlike the *Mary Celeste* in size and rigging as near as Ellis could tell.

"Who is it?" Ellis asked.

"Merrick, I should think," Silenus said. "Perhaps Margaret. We really don't know who won the Day between them. Whoever they are, they are falling further behind us. They cannot catch us now. We'll make the Gate before they can possibly stop us."

Ellis pulled the spyglass away from her eye.

"You've done it, Ellis." Silenus grinned. "We're free!"

"What about Alicia?" she asked.

His smile fell slightly as he looked at the deck.

"Silenus Tune," she said as she looked at the young man. "What about Jonas?"

He glanced at her and then toward the storm in the distance off the side of the ship.

"No," Ellis said, setting her jaw.

"Please, Ellis. Jonas came to get you out," Silenus pleaded. "He came to help you get Jenny out."

"No!" Ellis shouted. She started back down the length of the deck, moving quickly past the deck hatch cover toward the quarterdeck. "I'm not leaving him!"

"It's what he wanted," Silenus said, gripping her arm and turning her back to face him. "He knew the risks when he came."

Ellis pulled her arm away from Silenus. "You have *no* idea what risks he took or why he took them. *I* know! *I* know because I *chose!*"

She turned back to the ladder at the rear of the deck, pulling herself up onto the quarterdeck.

"If you do this, you put us all at risk, Ellis!" Silenus

shouted. "Not just us, but everything he tried to do. You'll make his sacrifice *meaningless!*"

Ellis ignored him. She strode to where Captain Walker stood at the helm. "Captain, steer to . . . to larboard."

The captain looked at her in horror. "Beggin' yer pardon, ma'am, but we're running with a favoring wind and we've no real crew to man the sails."

"You've got Ely here and Silenus to help you and Dr. Carmichael for that matter, for all the good he'll do you. Show them what to do and I'll steer the course."

"Ma'am, I think you had better just—"

"You'll never get out of the Tween without me, Captain, you know that," Ellis said in the firm voice that she had inherited from her mother and which she had used to great effect in the hospital wards with her "angels." "Follow me and you may yet live."

Walker considered this for a moment and then stepped back.

"Take the helm, ma'am. Steer your course and I'll do my best to keep the rigging in trim." The captain turned to the young man standing on the quarterdeck next to them. "Come with me, Master Ely, and I'll show you a thing or two about the sheets."

Ellis gripped the handles of the heavy wheel with both hands as Walker and Ely moved to the larboard rail.

"At your leisure, ma'am," Walker called as he put his hands to the lines secured around the belaying pins.

Ellis only nodded and started turning the wheel.

The bow of the ship swung to port.

They were heading straight into the storm.

"I choose," Ellis said into the gathering wind. "I choose us."

THE END OF PART TWO